MINTED

B. E. BAKER

Purple Puppy Publishing

For my darling Emerald

You always put people first, and that's one of the most amazing things about you. It's not showy, and it's not impressive, and it's RARE. Never lose that.

Also, without you, this story wouldn't exist. Thank you for loving my characters as much as I do. Your love can and does move mountains, even now.

BARBARA

Ten months ago, I saw my husband's favorite suit in the pile of our things that were earmarked for Goodwill.

"How'd you get in there?" I pulled it out, whipping it a time or two to free the wrinkles it had accidentally caught by being folded. I still remembered the time I spent haggling with the clerk—it was from the prior season, but it looked *amazing* on him. I managed to get the price down, down, down, until my husband walked out with the nicest suit I'd ever seen. . .for a price we could actually afford.

And now that same designer label was staring at me from our donation box. It felt significant for some reason.

"This almost got donated." I laughed as I handed it back to him. "Can you even imagine?"

Only, his chuckle when he took it and hung it on his side of the closet wasn't quite right.

A few weeks later, when I drop an earring and watch it roll across the floor of our closet and onto his side, I get down on my hands and knees and follow it.

When I stand up, my eyes are drawn to the rows and rows of suits hanging in his side of the closet. Plaid. Tweed. Grey. Tan. Striped. He has one of each, or in some instances, several. As a Brit, he can really wear almost anything and pull it off. Because he works in an office everyday—*our* office—he has amassed a metric ton of nice suits.

But the nicest one, the only designer suit he owns, is missing.

I wrack my brain to try and remember the last time he wore it, but I can't. I run my hand down the row, just in case I'm missing it somehow, but the one that I bought him for my mother's funeral is definitely gone.

I slide my earring in place, and I walk out of the closet to ask where it has gone. "Hey, is the suit at the dry cleaners?"

"What suit?" When he turns to face me, it's there again, the slight discomfort underlying his question. That's when I recognize what I didn't a month ago.

He feels guilty about something.

"Is something going on?" I ask softly, not sure I really want to know.

Will my question cause a fight? What happens if it does? Do I really have the bandwidth to deal with an argument right now? I'm nearly ready for work. I just need to grab my jacket and slide my feet into pumps, but he's ready right now. But I want to know where it is. . .and why.

It was expensive, sure, but more importantly, his dove grey suit fit him *just right*.

That's not something anyone would say about me these days, no matter what I was wearing. Nothing really fits me right now. Actually, I had to buy a whole new wardrobe after Mom passed, and then again a few months later. It's been a rough year. But my husband looks *flawless*—my amazing, handsome, debonair husband.

The one who won't meet my eye when I ask him about the suit.

He glances at his watch. "I better head out. I have an early meeting."

"Wait, you're driving separately?" I arch one eyebrow.

He nods. "Plus, after dinner I have that thing. Remember?"

"The fundraiser?"

He nods.

"Right."

"Okay." When he turns to go, there's no hug. There's not even a peck on the cheek. He just heads for the door.

That's the moment that I *know*.

I can't explain why I know. I'm not sure how it can be true. It wasn't a single moment or a single day, but in *that* moment, it hits me like a mallet to the head.

My husband's having an affair.

There have been too many *things* lately. There've been too many early meetings. And the most condemning evidence of all is the mysterious suit. Being in the donate pile a few months back clearly wasn't a mistake. It was there intentionally, and I was too obtuse to parse out what it meant.

I wonder how many other *things* I missed.

I'm still not sure why the suit was cast off, but it's definitely symbolic. I chose that suit. It was the one prize that came from this miserable excuse of a year. But now that I've recognized that something's off, I can't pretend, not even for a second.

That's just how I'm wired.

A moment later, I race after my fleeing husband,

barefoot, no jacket against the cold. To add insult to injury, it's raining outside, and when he sees me racing toward him, instead of being worried, instead of having concern for my health or fear that something might be wrong, my darling husband's jaw locks up. His eyes flash.

Because he's annoyed.

I wonder, in that moment, what caused it. Was it the weight I gained that changed his regard for me? Was it my chronic neediness over the last year, clinging to him like he was oxygen in a hostile, unfamiliar world I no longer recognized? Did I treat him like I treated chocolate, as a life preserver in the face of a terrifying flood?

Did my mother's death destroy us? Or maybe it was my father's, which followed closely after. If not that, was there something about me that would have destroyed us no matter what else damaged our bond?

The rain has plastered my hair to my forehead, my cheeks, and my neck by the time I reach his side. He still doesn't look concerned.

He looks *tired*.

"How many times?" I ask.

"What?" He's scowling now. "Barbara, what are you doing out here? Go inside."

"Just tell me how many times." Even to my own ears, I sound crazy. There's probably no possible way I could be sane in this moment.

"What are you talking about?"

My voice rasps the words, "How many times have you slept with her?"

I expect him to deny it. I expect him to lie, just as he's lied with every small action, with every story about a meeting that didn't exist, and just as he's lied with every missed touch and kiss he owed me as my husband.

I expect him to lie, straight to my face.

So when he doesn't, when he asks, "How did you know?"

It hurts *more*.

I start to shiver then, as the rain sluices between my neck and my blouse, as my unprotected feet are sliced by the rough shape of the malicious gravel underneath them. "It's true."

He sighs, finally pulling out an umbrella and holding it over his own head. "How did you find out?"

"It was the suit." My lips are shaking as raindrops hit them and run down to my neck. "You donated the suit."

"Maybe it was symbolic." He laughs, but this time he's not even trying to mask his frustration. "I tried to donate it, but you brought it back. So I threw it away," he says. "It's what I was wearing when—" He cuts off in disgust. "It kept accusing me, making me feel the same way you are right now."

He was wearing *my* suit when. . . "We're over," I whisper.

In the movies, couples argue. Every disgusting, lousy cheater fights for the love they've clearly already abandoned. The heroine retains a shred of pride, because the guy pretends to care that he screwed up. But not my husband. James just nods slowly, turns around, and gets in his car. He has a meeting, after all, and later today, he has a *thing*.

What he doesn't have any more, apparently, is a wife.

No, I've clearly been on my own for a while. I'm just so stupid that I'm finally realizing it.

❧ 2 ❧

BARBARA

When I was ten, I wanted to be a ballerina. By twelve, I realized that was never going to happen, and I decided to set my sights on becoming a pop star. Since I couldn't carry a tune, it only took a few months for that bubble to pop. I've changed my mind about my career more than a dozen times since then, and I've often started new jobs to follow my new path.

About eight years ago, I wound up working at a marketing firm that specialized in social media marketing. It's grown by leaps and bounds, even doing good business during the COVID mess. A lot of that was thanks to some initiatives I spearheaded, like bringing in micro-influencers who can grow our brands on a budget, and as they grow, so do our clients.

Sometimes it feels like the micro-influencers aren't worth the trouble. I've had two of them on a list for needing updated paperwork for months, but one of them finally came through. That means the only holdout account for year-end reporting is Twinning.

It's probably the cutest account we work with—two

wicked-smart eleven-year-old girls who are identical twins. We started working with them more than two years ago when they were only eight. They would play pranks on people—and catch them on video. When they revealed they'd fooled their teachers and had the same twin take both math tests, for instance, those videos really went viral.

I mean, they probably got in trouble at school too, but I'm not their mom. And people loved their content —the pranks they came up with were really impressive for kids. Always harmless, but always a hoot. It wasn't until they had a few viral videos that I found them, and now I have a big client who wants to work with them —a gum company that wants to do something similar to the old Double Double Wrigley's gum ads.

Retro is in.

But we can't set up any more promotions— certainly nothing like a commercial—until their paper-work is all set for next year. I shoot them an email asking *again* for the signed forms, and I say that I'll follow up with a call tomorrow. This kind of thing is routine for me—as the boss of the social media depart-ment, I make big decisions, but I catch little things too. I'm sort of like a mother in that way. Big ideas originate with me, and I'm also stuck doing all the small clean-up stuff. I've actually really liked most things about this job, but recently things have gotten a little sticky on a personal front. Sadly, personal and business have been inextricably entwined here since I married James.

In fact, I'm considering another career change just to get out.

"Hey, B. Have a minute?" No knock on the side of my door. No cleared throat. Nothing. Just starts talking.

"I asked you not to call me B," I say, aware that I sound a little juvenile, but unable to help myself. "What do you want, James?"

My stupid British ex-husband looks exactly as pristine as ever. His three-piece suit would look stupid on anyone else, but it works for him. So does the brightly colored tie and the perfectly coiffed hair with just a tiny line of grey at his temple.

By contrast, my hair's thrown up into yet another messy bun. I didn't bother with lipstick today, I have a small stain I didn't notice until I was already at work on the hem of my blouse, and I'm wearing boring, slightly scuffed, black flats.

Mostly, though, I hate how flustered I always feel around him.

He looks at me with an expression of condescension that I *hate*. "I just wanted to check in about the holiday party."

"Check in?" The office assigned the two of us to handle holiday party duty last December, back before we were divorced. No one even knew we were struggling then, so we agreed. Several of our biggest clients throw big parties, and we run some of them. Others, they just want us to attend. It's actually not too bad, usually. But now that we've been divorced more than six months, I kept hoping someone would think to reassign one of us so we didn't have to go together.

So far, no luck.

"I mean, do you really want to go to a half a dozen holiday parties with me?" He arches one eyebrow. "It's not that we can't, but it might be. . .awkward."

And the holiday season is officially upon us. Now that Thanksgiving's past, we have more than one every week. "Did you ask Doug whether he could take over?"

"He's leaving on a cruise that interferes with four of

the six," James says. "When I found that out, I couldn't bring myself to ask him."

Usually my ex is the nation's leading expert at imposing on people, even in bad situations. Or maybe that's just me—he's great at imposing on *me* in bad situations. "What do you want to do, then?"

"I think it'll be fine. It's not like we can't be in the same room. We've worked together here this whole time, after all."

"That's your plan? We should just both go?"

He cringes a little. "I mean, you could send Angela or Heather."

"Neither of them can handle the politics of attending—much less running—a holiday party."

"Well." He shrugs. "I guess we'll just have to suck it up."

I wave at the door. "Fine. Whatever. But I'm not going to walk around with you on my arm all night. People are going to know we're divorced, so get ready."

"Aye aye," he says, and then he salutes, like he thinks he's a Marine or something.

"Ooh, I'm glad I caught you both," Jennifer says from the doorway. "I wanted to go over something."

Our boss is unfailingly perky and she's not even thirty yet, but somehow she wound up with the quintessential name from our generation.

"Yeah?" Please, *please* let her be replacing me for the holiday party representative. That would make the next few weeks so much nicer.

"It's about the holiday parties."

Yes. I breathe a visible sigh of relief. But then my brain realizes that she doesn't look like she's delivering good news. She looks nervous. Like we won't like what she's telling us.

"A few weeks ago, we started submitting our RSVPs

to a dozen or so clients for their holiday parties, as you probably already know. It's critical at things like this for Follow to put its best foot forward."

I hate how every time she has to share something bad, instead of saying 'I' she says it's important for *'Follow'* like she *is* the company. "Okay."

"You two did such a dynamic job last year, going to represent the company together, and you each chair a different critical department, so I sort of submitted your names without thinking."

I already knew all of this. So why does she look nervous?

"We kind of figured," James says.

"Well," Jennifer says. "We did consider changing things out, but with Doug's cruise and Heather and Angela's relative newness. . . We felt a little stuck."

"Okay," I say. "Is that all?"

Jennifer scrunches her nose, and I can feel the bad news coming. "We typically send someone from each department."

Oh. A knot forms in my stomach.

"Barbara will be handling content marketing and social media, James will be there for public relations, and Kristy's our go-to for branding and design." She bites her lip and pauses before saying, "I wanted to see whether you two thought that might be a problem."

She wants to know whether it might bother me to attend a whole string of client holiday parties. . .with my ex and the new girlfriend he left me for.

Is this a joke? Or does she really have no idea *why* we broke up or that they're still together?

I mean, at the end of the day, I suppose this situation is really my fault. I should've found a new job, but with the divorce and marketing efforts for the holidays amping up, I haven't had much time to dedicate to it.

Plus, part of me really hates the idea that after *he* leaves *me,* I'm the one who has to leave. Like, why can't they be the ones to get out?

"It's fine," I say. "It won't bother me a bit."

"Great," she says. "And I actually RSVPed for four, just in case you want to bring a plus one." She beams, like that's some kind of gift. But it means she clearly knew that James and Kristy would be going together.

And now I officially hate her.

Since I don't have a plus one, I'm going to look even more idiotic. I force the word out through gritted teeth. "Perfect."

Which is why, instead of taking a lunch break, I spend that hour scrolling through my friends feed and making a list of people I might be able to ask to be my plus one. Making a list is probably the wrong phrase, actually, since I have about two people, and one of them is my best friend's husband. No one would have to know that Dave's married, right?

When I finally get off work, I'm starving. I'm *so* hungry after eating a granola bar for breakfast and skipping lunch that I do something I never ever do. I break out the emergency Girl Scout Cookie box. Thin Mints aren't exactly healthy, but I would eat literally anything right now. I rip open the silver foiled sleeve of cookies as I hit the elevator button, relieved that no one else is here, waiting to go down at six oh nine.

I'm running a little late, so I'm going to have to drive straight over to Seren's house from here, or I might miss all of Killian's party. There aren't many things in life right now that are zero stress for me, but being around Seren's family is one of them. Their family's a mishmash of broken people, but somehow their house still manages to be one of the most healing places in the country, I'm convinced.

I'm cramming the third cookie in my mouth when the elevator doors open.

James and Kristy are standing inside, holding hands. Both of them turn to stare at me, their eyes widening in tandem, like they're some kind of choreographed mime act. "Oh." Kristy's eyes glance down at the sleeve of cookies in my hand.

I whip it behind my back. "I missed lunch because I was planning—" I glare at James, chew, and swallow.

"I forgot my purse upstairs." Kristy giggles.

I don't hate her. I really don't. She's petite, and thin, and she's reasonably competent at her job. I try my hardest to be an empowered woman and not hate the woman just because my ex is gross and now she's dating him. But grown women should *not* giggle like they're teenagers. They just shouldn't.

I toss my head and wait for them to get out so I can get in.

They finally do, and they should be headed for her office. But as the doors close, I hear James muttering something. I don't catch all of it, but he's clearly making a comment about how he's glad we're not going down at the same time, because with me there, we might exceed the weight limit.

I want to punch him in the nose.

One of the best things about our divorce is that I don't have to hear his thoughts on my weight any more. But hearing him at work, mocking me to his new girlfriend? It really sucks.

By the time I get to the bottom floor, I'm bawling.

When I met James, I was a svelte size six with curves in all the right places. He came over to New York on a work visa, and he was the guy in the office that every girl swooned over. When he liked me, I was shocked.

We dated for several years—until a problem came up with his visa, so we got married. It made sense. He got to stay, and we could be together.

But then my mom died. After my dad died a few months later, I went from really, really sad to entirely depressed. I also discovered that when I'm sad, I eat. I ballooned from a size six to more than double that. I still run a few times a week. I still feel pretty good, unless I'm looking in a mirror.

Or being mocked on an elevator.

I did try to lose the weight, especially when James started saying that it bothered him. I tried Weight Watchers. I tried the keto diet plan. I even tried strange things, like the potato diet. None of it worked. The only thing that made me feel better was sweets, and the more James harped and complained, the more I needed to feel good about myself sometime. It was a very bad cycle.

Not that I've lost any weight since we broke up, either.

Once the holidays are past, I'm going to start over —calorie counting this time. But I just can't navigate work and holiday stress while eating nine hundred calories per day. I'll rip someone's head off and wind up in prison. Also, when I'm dieting, I don't have the energy to run, so I know it's healthier to lose some weight, but there are definitely trade-offs there, too.

I know all of that. I'm a smart woman.

And I'm still bawling in my car when I get to Seren's house. Which is why I sit outside for a few extra minutes and go in *really* late. My best friend Seren, unlike me, looks exactly the same as she ever has.

When we were young, I was the one who had the best figure—thin with a large chest. But now, she's still thin with a moderate bosom, and she looks elegant beside. My chest is sagging and my stomach is bulging, and if she weren't the perfect friend, I might resent her for it.

No one in the world could dislike Serendipity Colburn Fansee.

The second she sees me, her eyes light up and she rushes over to hug me. "When are you going to quit that job? You're working too much." She's wearing an apron, and I can smell the peach cobbler already.

"You made cobbler."

She shrugs. "It's Killian's favorite."

"It's a birthday party," I say. "You should make the boy eat cake."

Seren points at the table, and I notice a large chocolate cake, already covered with brightly colored candles.

"Bless you."

Because unlike James, Seren never judges me on how I look or what I'm eating. If she saw me eating Girl Scout cookies, she'd just hold out her hand for one. Depending on the kind, of course. She's absurdly picky.

"Barbara." Dave's smiling as he shoots out the hall. "Another responsible adult. Thank goodness."

"Where are the kids?" I ask.

Seren sighs. "Killian has been praying every day for nice weather."

I blink. "Does he pray?" The boy was an absolute heathen when they took him in.

Dave laughs. "Not really, no. But we told him that if the weather was nice, he could have the party in the back garden without any of us hovering. Apparently when you're turning fifteen, the idea of having parents or their friends standing around is scarier than talking about safe sex with your dad."

I laugh. "Do you talk about safe sex a lot?"

"The only safe sex is not to have it," Seren says, her face very intent.

Dave pulls a face, like they've had this argument before.

Seren says, "But hopefully none of that will come up tonight."

The front door swings open, and I turn, hoping it's Killian.

Instead, Bentley Harrison strides in like he owns the place—he does that literally everywhere. But he's as close to Dave as I am to Seren, so for about fourteen years now, we've been at every family gathering together. He's brought women with him off and on. I've brought a few guys too—most recently, James—but the two of us have always been here. Except for the months at a time when he was traveling, I guess.

Usually Bernie and his wife are around too—but I think they're at his in-laws this weekend. If I remember right, Killian's birthday is the same as Bernie's wife. He misses Killian's party a lot.

I'm actually surprised Bentley's here, too. He travels a lot.

"Back from Spain?" I ask.

"France," he says. "Better pastry, worse seafood."

I frown. "Does France really have worse seafood?"

Bentley shrugs. "Who knows? I hate seafood."

Classic Bentley. He's more of a meat and potatoes kind of guy. "So are you going back to Europe again soon?"

He shakes his head. "Actually, I was only there for five days this time. Earlier this year I hired someone to take over most of the travel for me. I only fly for really big meetings at this point."

"I bet that guy's not cheap," Seren says.

"The good people never are," Bentley says. "But in this case, it's a woman. She's a real battle-axe, and blessedly, she loves traveling."

"I thought you liked traveling," I say.

He shrugs. "I used to, but I'm getting older, and I'm kind of sick of it. I shouldn't have to leave again until January at the soonest, unless something goes wrong."

Something occurs to me, then. Maybe I could ask Bentley to be my plus one. Not as a date, but as a shield. He'll be around. He's an old friend. And he's not at all embarrassing. . .

He's rich, brilliant, handsome, and successful. That might actually be enough to offset the fistful of cookies in the elevator, at the very least. Now I just have to find the right time to ask him for a favor. . .

BENTLEY

Dave's family has always known me as the uncle who gives the perfect gifts. Since I'm going to Killian's fifteenth birthday party, the pressure is on. And right after that comes Christmas.

Ugh.

When I was fifteen, all I wanted was a car. Of course, I couldn't get one. Even back then, you had to be sixteen to drive. But he can get his permit soon, so maybe a car related item would go over well?

With their first kid, Emerson, it was pretty easy to think of things. That kid's always been a nerd, and he'd never had anything in his life. The bar was set pretty low. I think I brought him a scientific calculator for his thirteenth birthday, and he was giddy. Fourteenth was a microscope. Then a telescope. And when he could drive, I bought him one of those cop-detectors.

But they've raised Emerson, Beatrice, Jake, and Ardath. I had to find gifts for each. It was fine. I did it. But now it's Killian too, and with five kids to find presents for every birthday and Christmas, finding something unique and meaningful just gets harder and harder. Poor Killian has a birthday right before Christmas, so it feels even worse. I have to come up with two decent things back-to-back.

To make matters worse, whatever I buy can't outshine his parents. I learned that one the hard way, when I bought Bea a car. Whoops. Now I have to spend a moderate amount and yet still get something cool. What was fun feels almost tiring.

Maybe it's me. I haven't really found the holiday spirit yet this year.

I'm about to head over to their place when I start to second guess myself. My assistant told me that teenagers love headphones, so I did what I always do—ordered the most expensive option I could find. In this case, I ordered the Meze Elite Epoch headphones. They're limited edition and they look like something the *Jetsons* might have worn, so I figure that's good. They might cost more than whatever Seren and Dave buy him, but who would know? Headphones aren't something that *seem* super high dollar, so I should be fine.

But what if he hates big headphones? I've never seen him use any.

Is that because he doesn't have any, but wants them? Or is it because he just doesn't like the feel of big headphones over his ears? The whole idea starts to eat at me, so on the way to the party, I stop at the Apple store and grab him a pair of the new AirPods too, just in case. At least if he doesn't like either item, he can regift them, right?

Or, wait. Would he sell them or trade them for drugs? No, right?

Teenagers are hard, but foster kids are even harder.

In my experience, Dave and Seren have to do the

hard work. I'm pretty much fine to just buy the kids' love with extravagant gifts that Dave wouldn't buy. He has to worry about building character and maintaining authority. I don't need to do any of that. It's the reason I can take Killian out to shoot up a bunch of two-liter bottles, or take him for a driving lesson in my sports car. We usually just spin donuts, but as the cool uncle, that's fine.

The idea of being a dad is terrifying. Thank goodness I'm only the uncle.

When I arrive, no one's home. That doesn't bode well for a party.

Thankfully, they explain the kids are out back, pretending they're unsupervised. That means it's just Dave, Seren, and Seren's best friend Barbara in the house. I've known Barbara as long as I've known Seren, and it's always nice to see her. As a bonus, I no longer have to pretend to like her ex-husband now that they're divorced. I never like the guys she dates—she has atrocious taste—but that guy was the worst of all.

The worst thing about Barbara is that in spite of spending way less money than I do each time, she's my stiffest competition for best gift.

Which is why I find myself eyeing her bag.

"What?" she asks.

"What's that?" I toss my head. "Killian's gift?"

"Yes." She knows I'm competitive. She likes to irritate me by being obtuse. "It is his gift."

"You're a punk," I say. "Just tell me what it is."

"You'll find out soon enough."

"Actually," Dave says. "I'm not sure you will. I doubt Killian's planning to come back in any time soon."

"Wait, really?" I ask. "He's not coming in to see us?" I can't help frowning. "Then why did I even come?"

"Because you're showing your support to Killian,"

Barbara says. "Officially. But really, we came for moral support for Dave and Seren, and we came for the peach cobbler."

"Is that what I'm smelling?" I pull out a kitchen chair and sit. If they had a plate and utensils, I'd grab those too. It's always a mad dash when something comes out that Seren has baked, but with teenagers around, it'll be even worse.

Except, they're all outside, like chumps.

"Surely we'll get first dibs, right?" I catch Seren's eye. "How many of them are there outside?"

She laughs. "No more than a dozen. We made Killian promise to keep it small."

"And how much cobbler did you make, exactly?" I may sound greedy, but once someone has had some of Seren's dessert, they start acting the same way.

"Well, there's a cake." She points. "And I made three cobblers. That should be more than enough."

"I call the leftovers," I say.

"You can't do that," Barbara says. "That's not how it works."

I frown. "If you pull the 'my parents died and my husband left me' card one more time. . ." I shake my head. "You should have a punch card, and you only get special treatment twenty times."

"Well, my husband did leave me," she says, "and today, I found out that I get to go to a bunch of Christmas parties for our clients. . .with the heads of the other departments." She compresses her lips and widens her eyes. "Which includes him. . .and her."

"Wait." Seren drags a chair over next to me. "You don't mean James and Kristy."

Barbara nods slowly.

"That's crap," Seren says. "I'm calling your boss to tell her where she can—"

"It's fine," Barbara says with a forced smile. "Because Jennifer says I can bring a plus one." She pauses. "So, now it definitely won't be awkward." She groans. "I hate the holidays."

"You used to love the holidays." Seren looks so sad. Seren isn't ever supposed to be sad. She's like a Precious Moments figurine, or like, the angel in a school Christmas pageant. She should always be smiling.

"Quit your job," I say. "Come work for me."

"Because running away and imposing on an old friend's not pathetic," she says. "It's fine. Honestly. It's just work, and it's been six months. At some point, it'll stop bothering me." But she looks pretty bothered right now.

"I'm not sure that's how it works," Seren says. "Wounds don't heal when you keep rubbing salt in them."

"They don't?" Dave asks. "I think they do, but it's just more painful."

Seren swats at him. "Stop being a know-it-all."

"I think he's wrong," I say. "Which makes it worse. But you'll have to act more miserable than that to win the cake, Barbara. If that's all you've got, I can beat you."

"You can." She sounds disbelieving.

"You've at least been married—and engaged that other time."

"That lasted two months," she says.

I shrug. "Regardless. I've never been either. Better to have loved and lost than never to have loved at all."

"Oh, please," Seren says. "Nice try, but real pain is—"

"And it's her cake, so she gets to decide." Barbara's leaning toward me, already gloating.

"Look," I say. "There's a reason Shakespeare has lasted the test of time. The man was brilliant, and—"

"Dude." Dave shakes his head.

"Shakespeare?" Barbara's laughing now. "That's from Alfred, Lord Tennyson."

"Who?" I ask, intentionally goading her more.

"Only the most famous poet of the Victorian Era." Barbara looks way happier when she's being smug. With her arms crossed under her chest, she doesn't look like a sulking puppy any more, either. And all it took was one little intentional mis-attribution.

"Well, that Tennyson guy is also smart then, and that means I have the sadder case."

"How about this?" Dave asks. "I'm offering this out of the goodness of my heart, because I'd like to toss you both out on your ear, you beggars." He pats his stomach. "But as I'm officially on a diet, I'm willing to give *you* the leftover cake." He points at me. "And *you* can have the leftover cobbler." He points at Barbara.

"Swap those two and you have a deal," I say.

"Wait, you don't like cake?" Seren asks.

"No," Barbara says. "He likes anything, but he knows that I loooove cake."

I am rather chivalrous like that. "Now." I lean toward her and point at the chair. "Sit."

She listens, looking at me with a curious expression.

That's how I take her completely by surprise. "Yoink." I manage to snatch the bag right out of her hands. "Let's see what you got."

I'm *not* expecting to pull out a fifty-dollar Taco Bell gift card and a black beanie.

As soon as I start laughing, I realize I've made a mistake. Instead of laughing with me, Barbara looks embarrassed. "I've been working a lot, okay?"

I place the gift card and beanie back in the bag and

hand them to her. "Sorry," I say. "I think he'll love it. What teenage boy doesn't like Taco Bell?"

But she looks a little bit broken the rest of the night. Even when Killian comes in and opens her present and gushes and gushes, her eyes still don't sparkle. When he opens mine and flips out, instead of feeling vindicated, I feel small.

I'm hiding in the corner, scrolling through my phone, when Dave leans against the bookcase next to me. "Dude."

"What?"

"You're forty, man. You should know more about women by now."

"That's rude," I say. "I could have taken Seren from you back then, but I let you have her."

Dave arches one eyebrow. "Let me have her? Or knew that she already liked me?"

"I've been looking for Mrs. Right ever since, but all I keep finding is Mrs. Right Now."

Dave shakes his head. "Did you think some woman was going to show up and present an engraved invitation that said, 'Bentley's Future Bride'?" He snorts. "Think again. Life doesn't work like that. You're going to have to work for it."

"What does that mean?" I lean back against the wall, a little annoyed by the direction this conversation's headed.

"Are you dating?"

"Where would I even meet someone? I can't date someone at work. You saw what happened to Barbara."

"There are other ways," Dave says.

"Like what?"

"Online dating profiles for one," he says.

I explode away from the wall, more irritated than I usually get around him. "You've got to be kidding me."

"I'm not," Dave says.

"You never online dated."

"I got lucky and met Seren before I had to, but. . ." He opens his hands, palm up. "I'd hate to see you alone forever."

"Because marriage is so perfect?" I arch one eyebrow. "Tell that to Barbara."

"It's got its limits," Dave says, "but if you find the right person, yeah. It's pretty close to perfect." The soft look he has when he looks at Seren makes my heart contract. It's times like this, when I'm the loser who just can't find anyone, that really sting.

"I better head home," I say. "Early morning tomorrow."

"Tell your uncle bye," Dave shouts.

Even with his headphones on, half-dancing while talking to his friends, Killian hears his dad and steps toward me. He pulls one side of the headphones back. "Sick gift. Thanks, Uncle Bentley. You're the best."

I wave and smile, and then I'm headed for my sportscar. I finally got one that's not a Bentley a few years ago, and then I went a little crazy and bought two more. They're all actually pretty nice. As I climb into my McLaren 720S, I think about Dave and his doom and gloom threats. "What does he know?" I mutter.

But by the time I get home and walk into my empty apartment, I can't help wondering whether he's right. I'm over forty now, and I kept thinking I'd just meet someone. . .but I haven't. I'm still alone. I hate the idea of online dating, but. . . Was he right? Do I know nothing about women or finding the right one?

When I go over the whole incident with the gift in my mind, I have to concede that he might have a little bit of a point. Sulking in the corner after wresting the gift out of Barbara's hands might not have been a Prince Charming move, even if she's just a friend. I text Barbara, because I was too cowardly to do the right thing, but I have to do something.

YOU'RE A GREAT AUNT. I'M SORRY FOR SNATCHING THE GIFT AND MAKING YOU FEEL BAD, IF I DID. YOUR GIFT WAS GREAT.

She doesn't reply, which shouldn't surprise me.

It does surprise me when Dave calls.

"Hello?"

"So. You're home. Did you do it?"

"Do what?" I feel a little strange, like he has cameras on me or something. Does he know I texted Barbara? Is she still there? Did he see it? Are they talking about what a jerk I am?

"Did you look up online dating sites?"

I can't help my sigh. "Seriously?"

"Because I looked into them after you left, and for the record, it seems like if you want a match that ends in marriage, eHarmony is your best bet."

"Dave."

"Bentley, I'm serious. Look, you might hate it, but you can't say you hate pistachio ice cream until you've tried it, so just make an account and see what happens."

"Did you tell him they have a match every fourteen minutes?" Seren asks in the background.

"You told *Seren?*"

"We're both excited for you," Seren says. "We've been wanting you to find someone for years."

Oh, good. I'm a charity case, now. "Listen, I appreciate your concern, but—"

"Or," Seren says, "they have this one site called Millionaire Match, and you can find someone else who has a lot of money, too. They even verify—"

"That's my biggest problem," I say. "Half the girls I've liked turned out to only like me because I'm rich."

"Well, that's an easy fix," Dave says. "I'm filling out a profile for you right now."

"Dave, seriously?"

"They ask for income information. You can just say you only make two hundred grand a year."

"Why two hundred?" I hate that I'm curious, but now I'm wondering why that's the number he chose.

"Statistically speaking, women are way more likely to respond if you make more than a hundred and fifty, which makes sense. People want to have a decent quality of life."

"Then I should put twenty grand," I say. "That'll weed out the gold-diggers."

"And the good people too," Seren says. "If you want people who just want to get laid, then do that."

I groan. "I hate this. This is stupid. Surely you can see that."

"I guess we'll find out. . ." Dave says. "Bentley 1256. Because your account. . ." I can hear his fingers clicking on the keys while he hums the Jeopardy song. He finally quits. "Is live!"

"You have got to be kidding me."

"Nope. I'll text you the login info." There's a bing in the background. "Hey, you've already been matched!"

Two more bings.

"Wow, you've been matched three times already!"

I hear Seren clap and squeal. "This is so exciting."

"Hey, shut off my account," I say. "You two are weirdos."

"But I like watching it," Seren says. "This is so fun."

"I'm not sure how I feel about how excited you are

to see him get matched," Dave says. "Do you wish you were on there?"

"Hey, guys, shut it off!" I'm not entirely sure they're listening, but Dave does text me the information after I hang up. He shouldn't really know my email address and password, but when you've been friends with someone long enough, at some point you wind up sharing so they can look something up, and then they remember that your password is Igneous1234, for the poor dog you named while you were obsessed with rocks as a kid.

I sigh.

And then I log in to my shiny, new eHarmony account with a lot of trepidation. "What in the world?"

When I bring up the list of people it has matched me with—eleven already—I can't help noticing that one of them is someone I know in real life. Someone I've managed to royally tick off, even. This algorithm is clearly garbage.

Because match number six is Barbara.

❦ 4 ❦

BARBARA

I've known Bentley for fifteen years now, give or take, and I've seen him date a *lot* of women. One thing I've never seen is Bentley dating a large woman. I doubt he's even dated a size eight.

I'm a solid twelve.

Okay, fine, sometimes I'm a fourteen.

But it's not like I care about the number. Or that Bentley could never be with a woman my size. It's not like I thought I was really going to date him. I just thought he'd be a safe person to impose on as a meat-shield.

Until he made me feel like an idiot for giving Killian a gift card.

It's not like the teenagers at Seren's need anything, and I haven't had time to go shopping for the perfect gift. I shouldn't feel bad about giving him what I did.

Or maybe I'm not being honest with myself.

In that moment, when Bentley was lunging for me, smiling, and teasing me. . .it felt almost like he was flirting. I felt *special*, and I haven't felt that way in a long time.

But all he wanted was to open my gift, so I was the idiot for thinking he was flirting.

And his utter shock when he saw what I got?

I doubt I'd have been so upset about it if I hadn't had my hopes up for some reason. Which is stupid. I know he dates supermodels—he's stupid rich. He's smart. He looks like Liam Hemsworth. He's probably the prettiest guy in most rooms, even now, even a little older, at least, when Dave's not around.

There was no world in which I'd ever date Bentley, and I've always known that. So if I really was upset because I had stupidly been hoping he might, I don't know, turn around after fifteen years and suddenly express an interest in me? Shame on me for being an idiot.

My pet peeve is when girls write love letters to men who have been in their lives forever, confessing their feelings. They always seem to think the guy is going to magically wake up and be like, "Whoa! I never noticed you there, but now that you've said you like me, *shazam*! I find you irresistible!" It's nuts. There's no guy in America who has just been overlooking the girl who's standing right at his side.

I'm not delusional. If Bentley liked me at all, he'd have found some time in the past fifteen years to express his interest.

I do what any somewhat mopey, recent divorcee would do when her hopes flew high for no reason, but were painfully dashed. I change into pajamas and hop into bed with a bowl of ice cream and a slice of chocolate cake. The better part of an episode of *Emily in Paris*, and I'm feeling a little better.

The cake didn't hurt.

But then my phone buzzes.

I whip it off the nightstand, and it's a text from

Bentley. As if I didn't already know he was an unattainable unicorn, he actually *apologizes* for. . .what? Looking underwhelmed by my gift card? Openly acknowledging the silent battle he and I have had over the past decade and a half, in which I usually make each kid something special that's not very expensive, while he shamelessly tries to buy their love?

YOU'RE A GREAT AUNT. I'M SORRY FOR SNATCHING THE GIFT AND MAKING YOU FEEL BAD, IF I DID. YOUR GIFT WAS GREAT.

I never got upset about any of that before. It was kind of our thing.

But this time, he saw that he hurt my feelings, and he sent me an actual apology, with proper punctuation and everything. I slump down against the pillows. Even watching the rest of the episode in which poor Emily makes stupid decisions while inspired by a hot chef, I can't quite seem to get out of my funk. There might not be enough cake in the container Seren packed for me.

Normally, I'd call my mom in a situation like this.

And I know I'm not the only person in the world who has lost a parent. I'm not. I know that. I'm not even the only person who has lost both parents. But it *feels* like I've lost two legs on the stool of my life or something, and I'm not sure there's a way for me to get them back.

Eventually, I do force myself out of bed to brush my teeth and start the dishwasher, and that's when I see it.

A notification from stupid eHarmony—I haven't logged in for at least a month, but it's always sending me little teasers that I ignore. Only, this one is weird. Given my bizarre thoughts tonight, it's *really* weird.

"You've been Matched!" That's hardly surprising. The only being on earth excited about my social life is eHarmony. No, the surprise is the name it's listing as my match.

Bentley Harrison.

I mean, it's not a common name. How many Bentley Harrisons can there really be? In a million years, my friend Bentley would never ever *ever* get on a dating app. I've heard him talk about them and the people who use them.

I know this beyond a shadow of a doubt.

And yet.

Instead of ignoring the notification and finishing with brushing my teeth like a normal person, I swipe to open my phone and bring up the app. And then I'm even more shocked when I find myself staring at Bentley's gorgeous face.

I mean, he's not even looking at the camera, and it's a weird crop of the photo, but it's definitely him. Could it be a bizarre sign from the universe? Am I supposed to write him a horribly sappy letter about my unrequited love, get humiliated, and somehow discover something about myself?

No way.

There's really only one explanation.

It has to be a fake account. Someone stole his identity—probably some dork who works for him. They made an account with his information, hoping to use his looks and posh-sounding name to find a girl. I'd expect that more at like, Tinder or Match, but hey. People are branching out as women get smarter. I glance at the income.

Two hundred grand.

Ha! Bentley probably makes that in a normal *day*.

I think about just ignoring it, which would be the smart thing to do. There's no way that even a *fake* Bentley would be interested in me. But if it was me who had been hacked, I'd want to know that someone was impersonating me. I'd want to get a heads up or something.

I do the adult thing, even though it's a little hard, and I pull up his contact on my phone. It's ten at night, but he's the kind of person who probably swipes the silence notifications button on, right? If he's asleep, a phone call won't wake him up, surely.

"Hello?"

I fumble my phone a little and my heart accelerates. I guess I didn't expect him to answer. I've known Bentley forever, but I almost never call him. And when we text, it's about Dave or Seren. Always.

"Uh, hey. It's Barbara."

"Yeah, I got this weird thing—I think it's called caller ID or something. It tells who's calling me at ten at night so I can decide whether to answer."

"So, I know it's late, and maybe you won't care, but I wanted to warn you."

"Warn me?" Bentley sounds a little incredulous.

"Yeah, so I'm on this dating app called eHarmony, and I just got a notification that I was matched with someone."

"Okay."

"And it was you, only I know it's not you, because I know you wouldn't ever get on there." He's not saying anything. Why isn't he saying something? "Anyway, I think maybe someone from work like, took your photo, and they're imitating you so they can, I don't know, like, hit on people."

"Imitating me?"

"The profile's just awful," I say. "I mean, it made me laugh, but it's really, really bad. I doubt they'll convince many women to meet them, but they did say they had an income of two hundred a year, so who knows? Some women are really desperate."

"Barbara?"

"Yeah?" Before he can get annoyed, I cut to the chase. "Listen, I can email the web admin and report your account if you want, but I might need some kind of verification from you, like a photo of your actual ID to get them to take it down, and I'm not sure whether they'll give you information on who's doing it—like an IP or something."

"Barbara."

"Maybe you don't care, but people can google you, and if it were me, I'd want—"

"Barbara, it's really me."

"What?" I hate how shrill my voice sounds.

"It's my account."

Oh, no. Oh, no, no, no. I said—what exactly did I say? That it was bad. That the account wouldn't pull any girls at all. And oh, *no*. He knows it matched *us*, and that's how I saw it.

I can feel the heat flooding my face and neck. My face flushes really easily—a little bit of wine, the slightest embarrassment, and I turn into Sebastian the Crab.

At least he can't see me.

"Oh, well, neat. I guess, forget what I said."

"I thought maybe you were calling because eHarmony matched us." His voice is low, and it's rumbling in a way I haven't noticed before, and I realize that he's mocking me.

"Stop," I say. "But wait. Why does it say income of two hundred thousand? That feels like what a fake-you might put, just to draw people, but you and I both know that's way wrong. And not in the way people might think."

"Dave made the profile, actually, so I can't wait to tell him how terrible you think it is."

"I mean, it's not that bad." I try to backtrack. Why did I use such strong words? Ugh.

"I can tell it's not great," he says, "but I wouldn't even know how to improve it." He makes a hmm sound. "Yours is gorgeous."

Which means he thinks the picture from two years ago, before I had gained as much weight, is misleading. I mean, he's right. But it still stings. "Very funny."

"No, I mean it. You're pretty good at this stuff, clearly. Way better than I am. I have an idea, actually."

An idea? What does that mean? He's not suggesting. . .that we actually go on a date, is he? Why does that make my heart hammer in my chest? It's the dumbest idea I've ever had. When he didn't like me, I wouldn't be able to disengage, and every single event at Seren and Dave's would be a disaster from here on out. No, that must not be what he's saying.

Oh, crap. He's talking. Focus, you stupid, hormonal idiot.

"—could pay you, but if you could kind of hold my hand through this."

Hold his hand? Why did I zone out? Why was I focusing on the stupid hope that our match on a dumb dating site might mean something to him? Ugh. I blame James for leaving me an emotional mess. "Hold your hand?"

"I don't know how long it would take, but if you could spruce up my profile and help me pick people to date from the matches, that would be amazing."

"You want me to help you? Divorced and broken-engagement *me?*"

"What I hear is that not one, but two men asked you to marry them, and you have clearly dated seriously more than I have. Plus you have the inside track on women, right?"

"I do?"

"I mean, you are one."

My laugh sounds a little unhinged. "Right." *Get it together, Barbara.*

"I mean, I'm pretty busy right now with work stuff."

"Of course you are," he says. "It's the holidays, and you're stuck doing more work because of all the commercialization of Christmas marketing and whatnot."

"Right," I say. "But maybe we could try and get dinner tomorrow, and I can clean up the profile a little. Maybe look through your photo reel and find some other decent photos. Sites like these let you post more than one photo—I think eHarmony lets you post twelve. You want to do at least six or eight, because it makes it look less like a catfishing account."

"Like the one I have now?"

I can't help laughing. At least this time it sounds more natural. "Yes, exactly like that. An account where someone snapped a photo of the hottest guy at the office and they're trying to convince people that they're him."

"Are you saying I'm the hottest guy at the office, Barbara?" Why am I suddenly noticing how sultry he sounds?

My laugh's back to being super shrill. "No, I mean, I have no idea. I've never been to your office."

"Well, I'm going to take the compliment. Where should we meet tomorrow?"

"I'm not picky," I say, and then I have to suppress a groan. He's going to be thinking that what I said is totally true. You don't get as big as I am by being picky about food.

And now I want to crawl into a hole.

"Well, think it over, and we can pick something tomorrow. Maybe you'll have more cravings or something by then."

I realize that *this* is my moment. I wanted to use him as my shield earlier, and if my ex and his girlfriend watching me eat some Girl Scout cookies sent me into a tailspin, I definitely need one before I brave my way through all those holiday parties. "Hey, instead of paying me, would you have time to do me a huge favor in return?"

That's when I realize that he wants me to spruce up his profile. I'm asking him to spend twenty *hours* of his life with me—enduring boring work talk. Maybe asking for all the parties is overkill.

Right?

Right.

"Yeah? What can I do?"

"You said you'd be here during the holidays," I say, "and for work, I have to go to a few parties with my ex and his new girlfriend."

"Yeah, you said. That really sucks. I wasn't kidding about the job. I'm sure we could find you—"

"That's more than a simple favor," I say. "And you may think this is too much, and it's fine if you do. But I was thinking maybe you could go with me to some of them as my plus one."

Silence.

"Not as an actual date or anything." I cough. "But the thing is, just having someone there with me, a friend at my side, would help."

"Why not as your date?"

Now I can't breathe. Is he making a joke? It's probably a joke.

"I never told you this, because it would have sounded petty or jealous or something coming from me, but I hated James." He chuckles. "I hate him still, I guess. More, now. Before I just didn't like him, but now? I want to punch him. A lot of times."

"No punching at work things," I say. "Though if it happened in the parking lot. . ." I make a weird *Eh* sound.

Now he's actually laughing. "I'll keep that in mind. But listen, I'd be happy to be your date. Or to go as your friend, if that's better for you. Whatever you want."

He'd go as my date. Or not. Whatever *I* want.

Something must be wrong with my hormones, because I swear an image of Bentley in swimming trunks at the Hamptons flashes through my mind. I shake my head to clear it. "Really? That would be amazing. I have a *lot* of parties to attend, but if you could just do a few of them, I can just say you have conflicts on the others, and I won't feel nearly as self-conscious."

"The beauty of owning your own company is that any conflicts I have, I can remove. Just text me when they all are, and I'll clear my calendar."

Holy holly. I just landed the hottest date in New York State for what I thought was going to be the most miserable Christmas of my life.

BENTLEY

My mother had this purse—a Birken—that she loved. It was the right size. It was the right color. It had pockets for all the things that needed pockets. She would rave about it to friends, to family, and to neighbors. Of course, part of that was because it was limited edition, and she had one of only one hundred that were ever made.

I'm pretty sure she liked that bag more than she liked me.

I wish that was a joke.

To my parents, I've always been a bit of an accessory. To my tutors, I was a nuisance they were paid to teach. To my teachers, I was a scary problem—if I got bad grades, my parents who paid their tuition complained. To my coaches in sports, I was a tool to help them find success. To everyone in my life, I was something to be used.

Except to Dave Fansee.

He was the first person who ever treated me like someone he loved—someone he actually cared about. He saw me as a person. So while we were growing up, he always thought that I had the good life. But when I went to eat dinner at his house, I would bask in the shiny, warm love of his rambunctious and affectionate family every second I could before I went back home.

I know.

Poor, little rich boy. My parents always provided the very best for me, and I'm not someone who spent a lot of time complaining. But when everything you eat is a carefully prepared and executed meal made by a Michelin chef. . .sometimes you just want a Big Mac.

Now, at forty-three, I'm looking around at my life, and I'm beginning to think that the reason I've never found my Seren is that I've been going about looking in entirely the wrong way. Dave wasn't even looking when Seren fell in his lap, so I thought I could do the same. I would just live my life, and she would simply find me.

Did you think some woman is going to show up and present an engraved invitation that says, 'Bentley's Future Bride'? Dave's words keep rattling round and round in my brain. I mean, obviously I didn't think some woman would show up with my name in blinking lights. I didn't think it would be that obvious.

But I had been hoping I'd just meet her, and BAM. It would be clear that we were meant for each other. That reminds me of how *not* obvious it was to Dave when he met Seren. He wasn't looking, so he didn't see. I had to shove his face in it.

So if I have to do a little work, at least this time I'll have a competent guide.

Translator might be a better word for Barbara. For the first time, I have a secret weapon. Barbara's going to be my translator for all things female. Maybe she'll pick up the cues I've been missing and help me find the right kind of girl, too.

When I swipe to open the eHarmony app, I'm

prepared for double or even triple the matches I had last night. Thirty women as potential options that Barbara can help me work through, and guide me in messaging.

I'm utterly unprepared for two-hundred and eighty-seven matches. I nearly throw my phone.

I'm worried that Barbara will change her mind. There's no way that helping me—a remedial dater—and trying to work through this massive pile of misery will be equal to me going to a few holiday parties and eating some red and green appetizers while we make small talk.

She's going to quit, and I'll be back to square one.

I text her. HOW WE LOOKING FOR DINNER?

She texts back right away, thankfully. NOT SURE IT'S GONNA HAPPEN. CRAZY DAY, TURNS OUT.

Well, shoot. REALLY? I add a crying emoji.

COULD YOU MEET IN TEN FOR BREAK-FAST INSTEAD? BAGEL STOP.

It's a scramble, but I tell her I can make it. If my hair's not combed, well, she's my consultant. It's not like this is a date. Because I had to take Lucky out, I'm three minutes late, and she's already ordered two bagels—one of them with extra schmear. As always, she remembers the tiny details. That may be the most impressive thing about Barbara. She pays attention to people and does kind things without even thinking about it. She's wearing a suit that looks perfect on her—the light pink making her dark hair even richer, and her complexion light and bright.

"Thank goodness you squeezed me in," I say. "Because, look." I swivel my phone around and practi-cally shove it in her face.

She sets her bagel on the tiny table at the edge of the park we've staked out. "The world isn't fair." She shakes her head and perches on the strange high stool the city planners must've been drunk to order. "You know, I'd be lucky to get this many matches in a month, but slap up a decent photo for a guy and say he makes two hundred a year and this happens."

"Dave should have put a hundred a year, right?"

She's smiling when she glances up at me. "It wouldn't have mattered."

"What does that mean?" I can't help arching an eyebrow.

"It means your face is probably the primary draw," she mumbles, taking a bite of her bagel as she scrolls.

"I know you're super busy, so thanks so much for meeting me."

She sets the phone down and levels a stare at me. "I need to know exactly what your goal is."

"I want to be married this time next year."

Her eyes start scanning the area around me and not looking at me.

"Is something wrong?"

She snorts. "Well, about four women within earshot just locked in on you." She sighs. "Look, you can't just say stuff like that in public, not when you look like you do. And especially not when you pulled up in that Bugatti."

"Excuse me." A woman with dark hair and sunglasses bites her lip and steps closer.

"Yes?" Barbara says.

"I just wanted to see whether you wanted a coffee. I could grab you one." She shoots a frosty gaze at Barbara, and I realize she's asking *me*.

"Um, no. I don't drink coffee much. Upsets my stomach."

The woman frowns. "A juice then?"

Was Barbara serious? Is this woman hitting on me because I said I wanted to get married? I reach over and take Barbara's hand. "I think my girlfriend might be upset if you did that." I force a smile.

The woman swallows awkwardly. "Sorry. I misunderstood." She makes big eyes at Barbara and walks off, finally.

Barbara yanks her hand away.

"Sorry. It seemed like a good way to get rid of her."

"Listen, if I know your goals—what kind of girl you're looking for—then I can help you narrow these matches down. We can also fine tune your profile so that you're attracting the right kind of girl."

"No wonder you're so busy at work," I say. "You know a lot about this kind of stuff."

"Social media's my whole job."

"Whereas I'm a complete dope at it."

"It's become a little too much a part of our lives, I think." She pulls out a notepad. "Now, tell me what you want to find." She looks up at me, and I can't help noticing how cute her expression is when she's working. Her lips are pursed. Her eyes are alert and intent. She's so serious that I want to just. . .boop—touch the end of her nose.

Which is ridiculous. She's a competent businesswoman, a friend, and she's doing me a huge favor. The last thing I need to do is patronize her. "I want a girl who's smart. Competent at whatever she does."

She's scribbling, but she shakes her head slowly. "That'll narrow down two thirds of our applicants."

"Not seriously, surely."

"You're right. I'm being unfair and catty." She looks up. "And?"

"A sense of humor," I say. "Common sense. I don't want to date someone I'll also need to babysit."

"What's your age parameter?"

I blink.

"How young a woman will you date?"

"Oh." I hadn't really thought about it. "Thirty?"

She nods. "That's reasonable. It will also eliminate a lot..." She picks up my phone, uses my face to unlock it, and then starts tapping. "Okay, when I select for some college, and when I remove anyone under thirty. . ." She swivels it back around. "Fifty-eight matches."

"That was like magic."

She shrugs. "It's almost like I've been online dating for twenty years."

I can't help my sarcasm. "So clearly it works well. . ."

When she sets my phone down, it looks like she's miffed.

"I wasn't trying to insult you, though. I just mean that—"

She drops her pen. "There are no guarantees in life, and certainly there aren't any in dating either, Bentley. If that's what you want, you'll need to talk to someone about an arranged marriage."

"Whoa," I say. "Calm down."

"Sorry." She picks her pen up. "Sometimes some of my divorce bitterness just. . ." She waves her hand through the air. "Escapes."

"Good to know." I throw my hands around too as if to dissipate it. "And for me, sometimes rich entitlement just sort of. . .bubbles over. When that happens, maybe just swat at it and we'll be even."

"Swat *it?*" she asks. "Or *you?*"

"Either," I say. "And you didn't ask about this, but

I'd really like to find someone who doesn't like me because I'm rich."

She freezes and looks up at me. "Bentley." She grimaces. "I'm not sure that—"

"That anyone will like me unless they know?" That's what I was afraid of. I'm a little pushy and a lot opinionated, and I only have a few friends. I'm pretty sure they're friends with me because they've known me for so long.

"No." She's smiling as she shakes her head. "You idiot."

"What?"

"Bentley, I'm saying that as soon as they meet you, they're going to know. So even if you pick people who think you're *only* making two hundred a year, as soon as you meet them, it's game over."

"Why?"

Barbara opens her mouth and closes it. "Well." She picks up my keys, which are resting on the table, and clicks the button. My Bugatti chirps. "You have at least three cars that cost over a hundred grand. And." She points at my cufflinks, which are diamond studded. "Or." She points at my jacket, slung over the empty stool next to us. You can just barely make out the Gucci label.

"Who looks at the tag on the inside of a man's suit coat?"

She shrugs. "People who make less than a few million a year don't buy Tom Ford suits. Or Armani suits. Or Hermes or Luis Vuitton dress shoes."

"I don't even go shopping for myself. I pay someone to pick things."

"That's another thing you really shouldn't say. Everyone else in the world does their own shopping." She looks serious.

"I knew it," I say. "I'm a remedial case, and you're rethinking our deal."

She rolls her eyes. "I'm not, but you might want to consider switching cars with Dave for your dates, and maybe buying a few things that are reasonably priced to wear."

I reach for my keys, to put them in my pocket, and she grabs my hand and twists so that she can better see my wrist.

"Bentley. For the love of—your watch costs more than most people's cars."

"It was a gift," I say. "And would regular people even know?"

"They'll know Cartier is expensive, or at least, the gold-diggers will."

I sigh. "Fine."

"You don't even know where to go shopping for cheaper things, do you?"

I hate that I have to agree with her, but. . .

"Look." She glances at her watch. "I was going to spend the morning—never mind. I can be a bit late to work, since I'll be at that holiday party tomorrow. So let's just go grab a few essentials, but then you have to give me a ride to work."

"Deal."

"I'll scroll through these fifty matches on the way to the store, and we'll look for a handful of winners."

"I'm not done yet," I say. "I want someone I click with. Someone who's easy to talk to. Someone who gets me."

"You'll have to meet them to find out that stuff," she says. "But what about activities? What do you want them to like doing?"

"Someone who's active and likes to travel," I say.

"Someone who has a career of some kind, but doesn't mind prioritizing family."

She freezes. "You want kids?"

"Don't you?"

Barbara sighs. "I do, but it may be too late for me. It's never too late for guys, I guess."

"Too late for you? You're not even forty yet."

"Next year," she says. "But I don't mean that. By the time I find someone, and we date, and we get married. . . Once we have a solid foundation, I'd be beyond forty by a wide margin, and it just gets harder and harder to have kids for women." She shrugs. "I'm trying to wrap my brain around the possibility that it may not happen."

"You'd be such a great mom, though," I say. "Maybe it'll be like a lightning strike. Maybe you'll meet him and fall madly in love."

"That would be nice," she says. "So far, that has never once happened for me."

"Me either." I stuff the last piece of bagel in my mouth.

She opens my phone again and starts filtering through women. She's not asking me to do anything with them, so I'm not sure. . . "What are you doing?"

"I'm ruling out the idiots and the flakes before you've had a chance to see their photo and decide to give them a chance because they're pretty."

I can't help laughing. "Isn't that important?"

"Sure," she says. "But let's find people who might be a fit and *then* decide whether they're attractive."

She's smart with this, that's for sure. We head for the store she rattles off, but she spends most of the drive over scrolling in silence. We're nearly there when she says, "Okay, let's meet our finalists, shall we?"

"Sure."

She makes a drumrolling sound, and after I park, she turns the phone around. "First up, we have Denise Chitton, a graduate in finance who works at an investment bank in the City. She's sporty—plays handball three times a week—she's witty—references Shakespeare in a clever way in her profile—and she's pretty." She holds the phone closer and swipes through a dozen photos.

She's not wrong. Denise is tall, lean, and makes a mean duck face. I can't put my finger on why, but I'm not excited. Still, Barbara looks eager, so I shrug. "Okay."

"She passes. Nice." She makes a note, and then starts typing on my phone.

"Whoa, what are you doing? Are you messaging her right now?" I try to snatch my phone back.

"Oh, no way." She clutches my phone to her chest. "You're not allowed to touch anything on this app while I'm your manager."

"Wait a second," I say. "I didn't agree to that."

She holds out the phone, but I can smell the trap. "What?"

"No problem. You can take over again for yourself."

"Oh, come on," I say.

She pins me with a glare. "Bentley Harrison, if you want me to find you a woman who meets all your criteria, if you want me to weed through the over-made-up and social-climbing masses, then you have to do as I say."

As a control freak, this does not come easily to me, but I see her point. "Fine."

"You will not open the app yourself."

"I won't."

She smiles, and I hate how happy it makes me. She may as well scratch me behind the ears and say *Good*

Boy. "Now, here's contestant number two." She swivels my phone around again. "Marcia Oppenheimer."

"That's a name," I say.

"Oh, who cares about that? If all goes well, it'll be Marcia Harrison soon."

"Unless she wants to hyphenate, and then all our kids will be named something like Kirk Oppenheimer-Harrison, and they'll hate me forever."

Barbara rolls her eyes *and* snorts, which is how I know I'm being the perfect amount of ridiculous. "In addition to being just lovely, she's also a stand-up comedian some weekends, and she's very well traveled. She also mentions that she wants a big family."

When she spins it back to show me photos, I can't help notice that Barbara's a little too excited. The petite little brunette is cute, but Barbara's *beaming*.

"Why are you trying to sell me on this one? She didn't threaten you with a bomb, did she?"

"Huh?" Barbara puts my phone down.

"Oppenheimer," I say. "You know, the bomb guy?"

"Actually, you might have been right." Barbara purses her lips. "You're going to have a lot of trouble winning people over if they don't know you're rich."

"That's rude," I say.

"Look, our third and final contestant is a librarian, and she's both pretty *and* charitably minded. She helps set up little libraries all over the area, getting people to donate the books their kids have already read. She lists her passion as increasing literacy in children in the inner city."

"That sounds super duper fake," I say.

"What? Why?"

I sigh. "Who really cares about helping a bunch of people they've never met?"

"She likes kids." Barbara holds up one finger. "She's

smart." She holds up a third. "And look." She spins the phone around, and I can't argue with her. The librarian's lovely to look at. She's tall and thin, and her long, blond hair falls like a waterfall down her back.

"Isn't it strange that a librarian has photos that look like she's a print model?" I ask.

"Or a runway model," Barbara says. "It says she's five foot eleven."

"I like tall women," I say. "But I don't love people who are constantly staring at mirrors and redoing their lipstick. It's tiring."

Barbara's pretending to scribble something down. "Effortless beauty that is never annoying and never takes up any of Bentley's precious time." She looks up. "Sorry. I forgot to write that one down. You now have *zero* applicants who are viable."

"On eHarmony," I say.

She chucks her wadded up napkin at me. And then she throws the pen.

"Look, all I'm saying is that there must be some kind of balance. All those women look airbrushed and fake, and I wouldn't be surprised if half of what's in their profile isn't even true."

"And that, my dear Bentley, is online dating in a nutshell. Filtering out the lies from the truth."

How tiring.

"You better get ready," she says. "Because you're about to buy a fake wardrobe so you can fight fire with fire." She points at the door to the store and tosses her head.

Oh, no. She's right.

❧ 6 ☙

BARBARA

When I was little, we had this family that we hung out with all the time. My parents invited them over for almost every big holiday. Christmas. Thanksgiving. Easter. Birthdays. They had a little girl my age named Harriet, and she and I were close friends.

As close as you can be when you're eleven, I suppose.

Anyway, she was super nice, she was funny, and she was smart, too. Family get-togethers were the only time I ever saw her, since we went to different schools. But then as we got older, our elementary schools fed into the same junior high.

I was so excited that Harriet would finally be a school friend. As a somewhat awkward kid, I didn't have a ton of friends in my classes. If only we got the same classes, I'd have a bestie.

Finally.

On the first day of school, I hit the jackpot.

Harriet was in four of my six classes! She was a little quiet the first day and barely acknowledged that she saw me, but I knew that once things settled in, it would be amazing. Only, the second day, when I tried to sit by her, she told me the seat was saved.

Saved!

And not for me.

By the third day, it was clear she was planning to act like she didn't even know me. It broke my little heart, and I was also confused. I was *so* confused that I didn't even tell my parents. When my birthday party rolled around a month later, I expected her to skip it.

But she showed up, with exactly the present I wanted: a huge art kit.

"What's going on?" I asked. "I thought we weren't friends."

"Why would you think that?" She looked genuinely confused. "I really like you."

"But you ignore me at school," I said, even though it felt worse than that. It felt like sometimes she was even mocking me behind my back.

"Oh." She waved her hand dismissively. "That's just school. I didn't realize you were such a dork there. And anyway, it's too late to fix it now."

"It's not too late," I said. "If we ask Miss Kent, we can trade seats."

"No." She frowned. "It's too late for you—no one likes you. But we're still friends here, where that kind of thing doesn't matter."

That night, I told my mom what was going on, and she stopped inviting their family to our house for any gatherings. I've always wondered whether I did the right thing, or whether Harriet was right. Can you really separate your true feelings from your social act? Did I lose a true friend because I couldn't manage a basic human social function?

I mean, we all put on fronts.

And now, I'm helping Bentley put on the dumbest front of all time. I watch, in awe, as he goes into the dressing room wearing four thousand dollars' worth of clothing and emerges wearing two hundred.

"That belt is so wrong." I can't help laughing.

"Why?" He bends over, trying to see the belt.

"Never mind. It looks alright." I laugh more. "And those pants." I intentionally picked the ugliest clothes I could find at first, but I thought he'd filter them out. Instead, he marched out dressed like a British caddy for a pro golfer. Apparently when you don't shop for yourself, you just dress up in whatever someone hands you, like a living doll.

The worst part is that, even with loud plaid pants and an ugly sweater, Bentley still looks like an ice-cream sundae with extra cherries.

This deal we made seemed like a good idea, but now it feels like I'm just torturing myself. I've always known he was too good for me, but now I'm actively involved in setting him up with women who are dozens of leagues ahead of me, and the more time I spend with Bentley, whom I previously only saw at Dave and Seren's parties, the more I like him.

This could turn out worse than the Harriet debacle if I'm not careful.

While he's inside trying things on, I check my email to make sure I'm not missing anything critical. I almost scream when I see that I have another inane email from the HR department about the Twinning girls. Our client's going to be ticked if we can't set up the details of the holiday campaign in the next two or three days.

I open the email—which is essentially some complaint that the signature on the forms is nothing like the signatures from last year. "Do they think people are robots?" I mutter to myself. "My signature looks different every time." I click on the attachments, and I suddenly understand their frustration.

The signatures aren't just different. The signatures are *nothing* alike. One looks like an adult's quick scrawl, and one looks like. . .well, it looks like the little girls tried to forge it for some reason. And they didn't even do a good job. I sigh and fire off a quick reply. I'll have to go out for a face-to-face visit tomorrow. I'm lucky they're local.

But then Bentley's out again, and I'm distracted. Within half an hour, we've found some decent options, and while he doesn't look quite *as* yummy, he still looks pretty good. "Yes, those pants and those shirts are all interchangeable," I say. "That's the good thing about cheap clothes. They're made to go with most anything."

"We should get something for you," Bentley says. "To thank you for helping me." His eyes widen. "But we don't have to get something cheap." He looks around with an expression that makes it clear that to him, Macy's is like a Goodwill. "We could go to Saks."

"Bentley." I wait until he's looking at me. "I shop here. All the time."

"Oh." He shakes his head. "Of course you do." He cringes. "I need to not say stuff like that, right?"

"People who don't know you won't realize you're a benign snob," I say. "They might mistake you for a malignant one."

He laughs. "And I can't go around being cancerous, can I?"

"It would be better if you didn't." I glance at my watch. "Any chance you can drop me off right away?"

"You don't have time to pick a dress or some shoes?"

Shopping with Bentley? Telling him what size I'm wearing—a twelve with major muffin top or a fourteen—and trying things on while he studies me to see how they look?

I would rather hop up on a grill and barbecue myself.

"That's a pass for today, sadly. But thanks for the offer."

"If you're sure."

"I'm very sure," I say. "But I'm glad we found some things for you."

After I tell him where my office is, and he puts it into his GPS, he pulls out his phone and dials Dave.

"Hello?"

"Hey, man," Bentley says. "How'd you like to switch cars with me for a week or two?"

"Yeah, I can't do that," Dave says. "I know most people would probably kill for your McLaren or Bentley or that sweet new Bugatti, but I like bigger cars."

"The Bentley's not too small."

Dave laughs. "Dude."

"Or you could borrow the Porsche."

Dave chuckling. "You have a problem."

"It's only a problem if I can't afford it."

"Well, I have a teenager, and I can't give him rides to or from anywhere without a decent-sized back seat."

"He can sit in the front," Bentley says.

"But then where will Seren sit?"

"You can go without her," I say.

"Why on earth would you want to borrow my Acura, anyway?"

"Never mind." Bentley hangs up.

"Uh oh," I say. "What're you going to do? None of

those cars are something that someone who makes two hundred grand would drive."

Bentley sighs.

"Fine. If you *insist*—"

But Bentley's already typing something into his GPS.

C. A. R. D. E. A. L. E.

"Please tell me that you aren't about to *buy* a car so you can look like a regular guy."

"Because that's so much stranger than buying all those clothes?" Bentley looks absurdly handsome when he looks over at me, his eyes flashing.

"It's not necessary," I say. "You can just borrow my car."

"You have a car?" He frowns. "Then why am I taking you—"

"Mine's at the shop, but it'll be done today. I had to redo the brakes."

"Oh." His brow furrows. "What kind of car is it?"

"It's a Buick LeSabre," I say, lifting my nose just a little.

"A *Buick*?" he asks. "Are you serious? I thought you had to be fifty or older to even buy one."

"Well, the person who bought it was." My eyes drop to my hands.

"Oh." His hands grip the steering wheel a little too tightly. "I'm sorry."

"I should sell it, I know," I say. "But Mom drove it for years, and honestly, it kind of smells like her a little."

"It does?"

"Well, I keep buying the same air freshener she used, so yes."

He laughs. "Good call. That's not something you

could do with any other car." But the judgment's gone from his tone.

"I hate to play the dead mom card, but sometimes it comes in handy."

"Still, do you really think a Buick LeSabre is the right impression for me to make?"

"I think it won't scream that you're rich, and if you hit it off, you won't have to explain to the girl that you *bought* a car you had no interest in driving so you could deceive her."

"Interesting. I never thought of it like that."

"Your clothes are nondescript, so I doubt she'll even think about them if you hit it off. But a *car*? At least you'll be able to say you just borrowed one."

"Alright, alright," he says. "I get it. I'll borrow yours."

"Which of yours are you going to loan me?" The perks of this job just keep improving.

"Which one do you want?"

"This one's pretty nice." I run my hand down the armrest, and I sigh. "It doesn't smell right, though. Do you think they'd have the mothballs and old mice nests air freshener at the corner store over there?"

"No air fresheners allowed," Bentley says.

I'm laughing as I get out of his car. "Don't worry. I'm sure once I've spilled a few sauces from Chick-fil-A, it'll smell just fine."

He's cringing like he's not sure I'm kidding. Which is exactly what I want. "When's the first holiday party?"

"Oh, shoot," I say. "I forgot to text you." I cringe a little. "It's tomorrow. Can you still come?"

"For sure," he says. "Text me the time. We can change cars afterward."

"Right," I say. "Good plan."

"What should I wear?" he asks.

"Not your undercover stuff. I want you to knock everyone's socks off."

"Knock socks off," he says. "Check."

"I'll be wearing a bright green dress."

I'm about to go in when he freezes. "Oh, no."

"What?"

He flips the phone toward me. "Someone sent me a reply." He swallows. "Why does it say a *reply?*"

"I messaged them, remember?" I gesture for the phone. "Gimme."

He hands me his phone, and I pull up the message. "Lila says she'd love to get to know you better," I say. "I think we go ahead and meet her. Yes?"

"Who's Lila?" He looks lost.

"Lila the Librarian," I say. "She was the most promising one."

"I don't think you told me her name, and I disagree that she's the most promising."

I tap a few things into the app, and hit send. "Well, I guess you'll find out the night after tomorrow, won't you?"

"Two days?" All the blood drains from his face. "I need more time to prepare."

"Trust me," I say. "You've had three dozen more matches since this morning. You'll have plenty of other options if this one isn't a love connection."

He nods slowly. "Plus, you can prep me more at the party."

I can't help smiling. Does he really think he needs to prepare? "If you two click, then you click, Bentley. It should be easy."

"Right."

I'm about to close the door when I hear my name being called.

"Barbara?" It's James.

I slam the door as quickly as I can and turn around, hoping Bentley didn't hear.

"I'll be ready with the numbers for the lunch meeting," I say.

"You're sure late coming in." He's craning his neck to look at the bright yellow Bugatti.

And the window rolls down. Bentley's leaning toward it so he's easy to see. "Hey, James." His two hundred watt smile might be a bit much.

"Bentley?" James does *not* look pleased. He never said so, but maybe he never liked Bentley either.

"I've got to run," Bentley says. "But I'll see you tonight, sweetheart." He kisses his fingers and throws his hand toward me.

I'm terrified that James will laugh, but he doesn't. His eyes bug out and his mouth drops open, and he splutters as Bentley's engine roars.

"You're dating *him*?"

"Don't want to be late for the meeting." I rush away as fast as I can, and during the meeting, I refuse to meet James' eye. Because this may be a lie that's just too big to pull off.

No one on earth will believe that I could be dating Bentley Harrison.

Nobody.

❧ 7 ❧

BARBARA

Normally, my makeup doesn't take me very long to do, because I don't wear very much. But when I'm going to a party for Clinique's management team, one of our biggest clients, I make sure to use only their products, and I take great care in application.

Unfortunately, that means I'm running a little late for the party.

Apparently James is too, because he knocks on my office door. "Hey, can you bring the gift? Kristy's meeting me there, and I'm not sure I can carry it by myself without damaging it." He smiles a little too smugly, and I realize he's fishing for information.

"I'm sorry," I say. "But there's no way that will fit in Bentley's car—any of them." I could shove the artisan holiday cake our firm sends every single year into the back of my LeSabre, but I don't mention that.

A muscle I used to love in James' jaw is popping, but instead of making me swoon, now it makes my lip twitch in humor.

Because it means he's ticked.

"You're not wearing *that,* are you?" His slow once over used to make my heart race, but now it makes me feel about as attractive as a toad.

"I am, actually." I stand up and smooth the lines in my green dress. "Or did you think that when we divorced, I'd stop wearing Boden's holiday dresses?" This one is A-line, and I think it looks pretty good on me, even when I'm, well, my current size. It's thick fabric, so it looks smooth, and it makes my ample curves look even more pronounced.

"Dynamite."

He says that all the time, and now I can't stand it. I frown.

"I guess I'll try and figure something out with the cake."

It's not in my nature to let someone struggle with something. I know he could call Kristy and make her come up the elevator to help him, but with my luck, I'd probably run into them again, and then someone would trip, and I'd end up face-planting into a two foot by two foot cake.

I groan. "I'll help you get it down, at least."

"That's something." James has never been the kind of person to hand out fake gratitude. I used to think it was refreshing. Now I just think it's rude. It's funny how your perception changes when you're not wearing rose-colored glasses.

Unfortunately, there's really no way to carry the cake without both of us facing one another, our hands braced on opposite ends. "Who came up with the cake idea in the first place?" I ask. "It's stupid. Why can't we have something delivered, like tins of nuts?"

"Or a big barrel of popcorn," James says. "People love popcorn."

"Once, that copy company sent us all custom notepads with fancy highlighters," I say.

"I remember," James says. "I think I still have the highlighter."

"Anything would be better than this."

"If our CEO had to lug this thing to a single party," James says, "you can bet we'd be sending a fruit basket next year."

It may be the first time I've chuckled around him since the divorce. I suppose shared misery can be a decent bridge. When the elevator opens on the garage floor, Bentley's standing there, awkwardly ignoring Kristy.

"Oh," James says. "You're here."

Kristy's glaring at him. "Looks like you two are having a lovely time. Did you coordinate those outfits?"

It strikes me then, that instead of insulting my appearance, James might have been annoyed because the green stripes in his tie exactly match my dress. My bright red coat and matching high heels are the exact color of the counterstripe, so. . .

We look like a couple.

And last year at this party, everyone at Clinique knew we *were* a couple. This might be even more awkward than I realized.

"We didn't," I say.

"No way," James says.

But we're joined by a cake box, and now we've stood still, both of us horrified, for so long that the elevator door starts to close.

Bentley dives in, blocking the doors with a martial-arts-esque move.

"That was so cool," Kristy says.

"Here." I shuffle out of the elevator, forcing Bentley back, and then I toss my head for Kristy to take the cake. "We can't take it. There's no way it'll fit in the McLaren."

"You drive a McLaren?" Kristy's eyes are round as saucers as she takes the cake box from me. "I thought you drove some crappy Buick."

"I just bought it for her." Bentley tosses me the keys. "She still has the Buick—it was her mom's—but I thought she needed something more fun to drive around town."

Kristy's mouth drops open and stays that way.

James practically wrenches the box from her, pulling her toward his older model Lincoln Towncar. "We'll see you there."

"Wait, I didn't even know you were dating anyone." Kristy's eyes are ping-ponging from Bentley to me and back again. "How did you two even meet?"

Bentley slings his arm around my shoulders. "I've known Barbara for almost fifteen years, but it wasn't until your boy over there messed up that I saw my window. It's hard to catch Barbara, between all the guys who like her, but I finally did."

I practically drag Bentley to the McLaren and point. "Get in."

"Whoa there," he says. "You look ticked."

"You think?" I climb into the passenger side without thinking and pass the keys back to him.

"I thought I was supposed to irritate them. No?"

"You *gave me* a McLaren?" I roll my eyes.

"You're going to be driving it."

"For a few weeks, tops," I say. "And then what do I say?"

"It got bad gas mileage?" He shrugs. "Why does it matter? Deal with that then."

I groan. "This is my actual life, Bentley."

He sounds contrite. "I know it is."

"It's not a joke, and when you go so over the top, no one will ever believe it. That's why I told you we should go as friends."

Bentley has just turned the car on, but he doesn't put it in gear. He turns to me instead. "Hold on a minute."

"What?" I tap on the clock in the display. "We're already late, though, so let's not hold on for too long a minute."

"There's no such thing as a long minute," Bentley says. "All minutes have sixty seconds."

"Wasting time," I say.

"What did you mean, '*that's* why you said we should go as friends?'"

"Huh?"

"What's why?"

"I'm confused." I mean, I'm not really. I know what he's asking, but I'm not about to tell him that I didn't want to go as his girlfriend because no one on earth would believe he and I could ever actually date.

It sounds too pathetic, even to me.

"Why would no one believe that we're more than friends?"

Aw, crap. He's not letting it go. "Because," I say.

"Because?" He lifts both eyebrows and waits.

Painfully.

Is he that obtuse? "Do you really not know, Bentley?"

He frowns. "No."

"Because. . ." That's when it hits me. He's obtuse, so I can lie about the real reason and avoid an awkward interchange. "Because you're such a player. James knew you, right? While we were married, he saw you with a different woman at every event."

"I almost never brought women to the parties and dinners."

"But sometimes you did," I say.

"I guess it wasn't ever the same person." He's still frowning.

"Knowing you, they're not going to believe that you'd suddenly start dating someone seriously." Phew. There it is.

"That may be the saddest thing I've ever heard."

For a moment, I feel a little bad. Am I going to give him a complex because of my own insecurity? But I shake it off. There's no way someone as confident and put-together as Bentley would lose sleep over people thinking he's a player.

Guys love that kind of thing.

"Well, we'll show them tonight that it's ridiculous," he says. "I'll be the most devoted man who ever took his girlfriend to a holiday party." He's now racing down the road with a huge smile on his face. He looks even more gorgeous than usual, and I may have created another problem.

Because if he keeps acting like that, I'm going to be screwed.

I'm pretty sure I'm already developing an unrequited crush. How do I keep my brain from running amok? I remind myself that he's just paying me for my services. I'm basically his employee.

And tomorrow night, he's taking Lila the Lurid Librarian out to dinner. . .and maybe more.

That's like a bucket of ice water to the brain.

"Maybe we should talk about tomorrow," I say.

"What about it?" Bentley's frowning, his eyes still on the road.

"Where are you going to take the lovely Lila?"

"Is that really what you want to talk about?" He

presses a few buttons until "I'm Dreaming of a White Christmas" floods the car. "There, that's better."

"What about that place—"

"Maybe Gabriel Kreuther. I went with Dave and Seren last week, and Seren loved the desserts." Bentley asks, sounding brusque.

"The new French place?" I whistle. "I hope that's a joke. You can't take her to a place like that. If Seren likes the dessert, it's out."

"Why?"

"Do you think Mr. Regular would go someplace that costs a hundred dollars a plate?"

He sighs. "I was excited to be dating in earnest at first, but this is getting tedious."

"Did you think it would be easy?" I ask. "You're rich and sophisticated and you want a woman who's smart, funny, gorgeous, and kind, and you don't want her to know that you're rich."

"You make it sounds like I'm perpetrating some hoax," he says. "I'm just trying to change things up a little so I don't date the same women I've dated unsuccessfully for twenty years."

"I think that's smart," I say. "But you can't just dial it in. Where's the best taco place you've ever been?"

He doesn't even hesitate. "Los Taco Number One."

"Okay, then that's where you'll go."

"They only have tables outside."

I snatch his phone from the center console. "I'll tell the librarian to dress warm."

"Will she do it?"

"Probably not," I say. "First date—she'll want to wear something slinky that shows how thin she is."

"You'd never do that."

His words hit like softballs, lobbed at my tender parts. "Rude."

"What?" He looks horrified. "How was that rude?"

"I'd never wear something slinky, because I can't show off how thin I am?"

Bentley slams on the brakes and pulls off on the side of the road. Then he turns toward me, his eyes wide. "Barbara, please tell me you're kidding."

I'm looking up so the tears that are threatening can't ruin my makeup.

"I meant that you'd never dress up on the first date to try and make sure the guy was distracted by how hot you looked."

That pisses me off more. "What do you think I did on the very first date we ever had?"

"What?"

"When you were being set up with Seren, and I was supposed to be set up with Dave, and clearly those two liked each other, I was dressed up in my nicest dress, and I was trying to look as hot as I could. *Every* girl does that, even forgettable ones like me."

"Forgettable?" He swallows. "Look, you are not forgettable. And I'm sorry. I wasn't trying to upset you, not in any way." He exhales. "I guess that just comes naturally."

And now I'm laughing. "You sound just like my dad always did."

"Well, at least I'm in good company." He tilts his head. "But Barbara, you *are* thin and beautiful."

I snort.

"You're not, like, chives, but some guys like women who have curves—you're like edamame beans."

Is he really comparing me to vegetables? "That's just a nice way to say that some men don't mind when women are fat."

He's not laughing now. He looks entirely serious. "Men shouldn't mind when women are fat—society makes fat into this four letter word that it shouldn't be. But even so, that's not at all what I'm saying."

"Bentley—"

"No." He turns back toward the road, and then his hands grip the steering wheel tightly. "Have you ever met my mother?"

I shake my head.

"All her friends look like skeletons you might set on your porch for Halloween, and it always made her feel horrible. But she's curvy, and my dad loves her for it."

I blink.

"Those skeleton women. . . It's unhealthy. Mom has always felt guilty when she even looks at food, and I don't want anything to do with it." He turns back toward me. "You had a very hard year, so you probably feel bad about gaining some weight, but you should listen to this next part."

It's too late. I'm already crying.

"You are every bit as beautiful today as you were when we met back on that ill-advised setup. Do you hear me?" He's staring at me.

I nod and swipe at my cheeks.

"You look like you don't believe me, so I'm going to take a photo whenever I think about it tonight. And then I'm going to send them to you, and you're going to realize that you look stunning."

"Bentley, do not do that."

"I'm not lying," he says. "Your brain's the one that's lying to you. The media's lying to you, too. You look great, and you're healthy, and you should not feel bad about how you look. Do you hear me?"

I hear him. I just don't believe him.

But this time, I'm able to fake a convincing nod, at least. Enough to get us back on the road. I use the rearview mirror to wipe off and reapply my under-eye concealer and touch up my mascara, though I almost poke my eye out when Bentley exits the freeway. "Dude, really?"

"There was a tire," he says. "Sorry."

But then we're there. The party. And it's time to pretend that this Greek god is my boyfriend. Whatever he thinks, I brace myself for everyone at the party to believe that he's either an escort or that we're lying.

Which, of course, we are.

"This might have been a dumb idea," I say, as I climb out of his car.

But then he's standing in front of me, and he offers me his arm. "It was a brilliant idea, and I'll prove it to you."

As we walk inside the hotel, I can't help relaxing a little. There are enormous wreaths made of fragrant pine boughs and holly berries. A tall, brightly lit tree stands at the center of the entryway, and white doves tie everything together. "The best thing about holiday decorations are the lights," I say. "Why can't we use twinkle lights in our decorations all year?"

"If we did, you'd stop appreciating them," Bentley says. "No matter how beautiful, no matter how impressive, they'd just become more noise. That's how it works. Unless it's new, unless there's a change, as humans, we just stop looking."

"So to enjoy the holidays, we need the other eleven months out of the year to be dull?"

"Exactly." He nods. "You can't like sugar without also having salty stuff. You can't appreciate pleasure without pain."

"You're more of a philosopher than I expected," I say.

After following the signs to the rear ballroom, I try to intentionally relax a little. I won't be helpful to my company whatsoever if I act like a complete nutjob tonight.

"Barbara." The woman in charge of color makeup waves me over.

Why can't I remember her name?

"When I heard about your divorce," the woman says, "I was shocked. I thought you and James were the perfect power couple. I was actually ready to take that man down a peg." Her eyes lift up. "But." She widens her eyes and looks back at me. "You definitely won."

"Won?" Bentley asks as he finally catches up to us.

"I'm Tawnya," she says. "I'm the director of color makeup for Clinique."

"You're the—what?"

"Color makeup—it's like, eyeshadow, lipstick, you know."

"Not their skincare line," I say. "Or not perfume and that sort of thing."

"Gotcha," Bentley says. "Well, I know it was a rough year for our girl." He slides his hand next to mine and intertwines our fingers. "But I'm actually glad that James was such a monumental—"

Bentley cuts off.

James and Kristy are walking behind Tawnya, coming from the refreshment table.

Bentley waves.

"Let's not even talk about them." Tawnya giggles. "I want to hear all about *this* guy."

Oh, boy.

"Well, you're about to get your wish." Apparently, when Bentley's lying, he skews just a little effeminate. It makes me grin. "We met fifteen years ago, when I was set up with her best friend."

"You're kidding." Tawnya's talking so loudly that

several other people have stepped closer, and now they're all listening.

"So it's true?" the man who always sends over the contracts—Davis, I think—asks. "You and James broke up?"

Bentley nods slowly. "About time, right?"

"If I'd been sure, I'd have asked her out," the man I think is named Davis says. "But I guess you were too fast for me."

"Exactly," Bentley says. "If I've learned anything from my fifteen years of crushing on her, it's this. You have to move fast, or someone else snaps Barbara up." That's the second time he's said something that ridiculous.

"I guess I'll just have to wait," Davis says.

"I wouldn't bother," Bentley says, dropping to a whisper. "I'm smarter than the Brit. I'm not planning to screw up."

Everyone around us is now roaring.

When I glance over my shoulder, James is standing in the corner with Kristy, scowling.

"But when was your first date?" a woman I've never seen asks.

"You're not going to believe this," Bentley says.

"Sweetheart, maybe we should keep some things to ourselves." I squeeze his arm pretty hard.

"Oh, I think a story this good should be shared." Bentley bumps my hip playfully. "I was pretty sly."

"You were?" Tawnya's biting her lip, her eyes bright. "How?"

"I told her I needed help finding someone to date."

Everyone gasps.

"She helped me set up my online dating account. She even helped me screen which women to take out."

"You're kidding," Davis says. "Why?"

"Because I wasn't sure whether she was over her ex." Bentley sighs. "And I was worried that if I asked her out too soon, I'd wind up being a rebound."

Luckily, the CEO arrives then, and our little court of lies is broken up by the planned presentation.

"You'll have to finish later," Tawnya says.

"Not if I have anything to say about it." I jab Bentley's side.

He glares at me, but he shuts up.

A moment later, my phone bings. I check it as inconspicuously as possible, assuming it's some kind of blistering text from James.

But it's not.

It's a photo from Bentley with one word. SEE? When I click the tiny icon, the photo downloads—laggy because we're inside a hotel, presumably—and I'm surprised.

It's a photo of me in my green dress and red heels. I'm half-smiling, and I don't look too bad. I mean, sure, my arm's at an awkward angle, so it looks thicker than I'd prefer, but I look mostly happy. Probably because I have a date with me, so I don't feel quite like the pariah I've been at work since James left me.

He did say he'd send me photos, but I thought it was just something he said. I didn't really think he'd do it. Once we're seated, as hidden in the far corner as I can be and still find two seats, I summon up my irritation at his blatantly fabricated story, and I let him have it. Quietly, so I don't interrupt the CEO's awards ceremony.

"What were you thinking?"

"I thought I did pretty well. When I'm forced to lie, I always stick as close to the truth as possible," Bentley says. "And in this case, that story was almost the absolute truth."

Which is why I hated it. It's a sidestep of what happened—the version of our story I wish was true, I realize. *If only* he had liked me for fifteen years. *If only* he asked for my help to find a woman as an excuse to spend time with me.

The reality is depressingly close in all the worst ways: Bentley's been exactly the playboy I've always known him to be, and he's asking for my help to find the perfect woman, because that's exactly what he deserves now that he's finally ready to settle down with someone.

I, on the other hand, am looking for the human equivalent of a Buick LeSabre. Driving a McLaren is just a ruse that's going to leave me very, very unsatisfied in the end. Basically, I'm playing with fire, and I'm finally realizing that I'm going to get burned.

It would help me a great deal if he'd stop sending me photos, but a small, stupidly-optimistic part of me hopes that he doesn't. And when I get home that night, I update my profile photo to the one he sent. I'd been avoiding updating it, now that I've gained weight, but he's right that I don't look *so* bad.

I just don't look good enough to be standing next to Bentley. Which is how I know it's not going to happen for real.

Ever.

✺ 8 ✺

BENTLEY

A lot of guys called Dave Garbage Guy when we were in school. A *lot* of them. It ticked me off, but it wasn't a problem I was equipped to solve. When I told them to stop calling him that, they'd ask me why. When I said it was because he was my friend, they'd just laugh or mock me, too. It always stirred up more interest and got more people to use the name.

The guy who started the whole thing was named Mark Bateman.

His dad owned a bunch of car dealerships, and he planned to inherit them one day. He didn't need to be smart, and he knew it. He never bothered to work hard, and none of the teachers had any sway with him. But then, one day, his dad's company had to file for Chapter Eleven.

Now, that's not something that most kids would even know.

Only, I read the news every day, and I saw that my dad was the judge handling the case, so suddenly, he had a lot of power over Mark Bateman. When his father realized who I was, he made a big deal out of it to me, telling me that anything I needed, his son would be sure to do.

I'm a little ashamed to think about how I behaved around Mark.

I made him follow me and Dave around carrying our gym clothes. I made him give us his lunch. I made him apologize to Dave, on his knees, even.

When I had the chance, I did not take the high road.

Because he'd been a huge bully, it was so freaking fun. I wish I could say that I regretted it, but I never did. I'm sure if I ever have kids, I'll have to lie about it. But last night, at that holiday party? It felt just like that. The funny part is that I didn't even have to do anything mean or anything I regret doing. All I had to do was show up and point out how amazing Barbara was.

Everyone can see her. They know she's smart, witty, hard working, elegant, stylish, and gorgeous. It was clear they had been gossiping about her breakup with James the Jerk. All I had to do was highlight what they already knew.

James traded in a sleek grey Ferrari for a bright red Audi.

Not that I think Barbara should be compared to a car. I feel bad even thinking about that. But still, the point is that she shone like the Christmas lights she so admired last night, and the only one who didn't see it was her. It was really, really fun tormenting her ex, and I liked sending her five or six photos.

But I have a new goal for the next few holiday parties.

I've learned a little bit from watching Seren. Twenty-five years ago, instead of making Mark

Bateman follow us around, instead of torturing him for making Dave feel small, I should've made Dave see that he was amazing, like Seren has. If I had done that, he wouldn't have been hurt by stupid taunts like 'Garbage Guy.' Last night, on our way home, I realized that James isn't the problem.

The problem is that Barbara believes the crap he fed her.

She should know that she's worthy. She should see that she's not at fault. Instead of making him feel low —which felt pretty good, I won't lie—I need to make Barbara see just how amazing she is. Then she won't care what James or anyone else thinks.

But I'll have to figure that out later.

Barbara just texted me. SEND ME A PHOTO OF YOU.

I make a duck face—which I'm absolutely awful at —and send it over.

NO, YOU MORON. I NEED TO SEE WHAT YOU'RE WEARING.

I WAS KIDDING, I lie. Then I snap a new photo and send it.

ARE YOU GOING TO PROM?

Huh? WHAT DOES THAT MEAN?

YOU CAN'T WEAR A SUIT. WE DIDN'T EVEN BUY A SUIT.

She's so cute. I'M NOT WEARING THIS FOR THE DATE. I WORE THIS TO WORK TODAY.

WHY WOULD I WANT A PHOTO OF WHAT YOU WORE TO WORK? WHAT'S WRONG WITH YOU? ISN'T THE DATE IN LESS THAN AN HOUR? WHY AREN'T YOU CHANGED?

I JUST GOT HOME, I text back. CALM DOWN. Then I plop down on the couch and let Lucky lick my face. Once she calms down a bit, I snap a selfie of me and Lucky and text that one too.

CUTE DOG, BUT GO GET DRESSED. NOW.

CUTE *DOG*? I text back. RUDE.

GUYS TEND TO GET UPSET WHEN I REFER TO THEM AS CUTE.

TRY ME.

OH, FOR THE LOVE.

YOU MISSPELLED CUTE.

YOU'RE VERY CUTE, BENTLEY.

And now I'm grinning like an idiot. So I go ahead and snap a photo of that and send it.

She thumbs-downs it and then says, GO. GET. DRESSED.

DO I HAVE TO SEND UPDATES OF THAT TOO? LIKE, THIS? I take off my jacket and undo my tie and send her a photo.

BENTLEY.

I'LL TAKE THAT AS A YES. I pull off my shirt and snap another photo. I'm just clicking send when her reply comes through.

DON'T MAKE ME BLOCK YOU.

I can't quit smiling. Once my suit is off, I put my 'regular guy clothes' on, like a good boy, and then I can't help myself. I snap a photo of the pile of clothing I tossed on my bed. . . And I send that.

Maybe her internet will be slow, and I'll give her a heart attack before the image loads. But will she be irritated?

Or is there any chance she's having as much fun as I am?

I feel a little guilty when I have that thought. She's probably still recovering from her divorce. She's a friend, and she's doing me a huge favor, and I'm what?

Repaying her by trying to flirt with her? She was upset at *pretending that* I'm her boyfriend.

Because she thinks I'm a player.

I mean, if I'm being honest, I guess she's right. I've dated a long string of women, and I've never really connected with any of them. Isn't that what a player is? Someone who's such a loser that he never really clicks with any of the great women he meets? It just always felt like the girls I dated were more interested in posting social media photos of our food and our outings than they were in talking to me, in spending time with me, or in listening to anything I had to say.

Not Barbara, obviously, but I've always followed my dad's strict rules there. No dating at work, and no dating among friends. It's too messy. It's kept my dad from ever having an affair, even though he's been married to a harpy for over forty years. If it can work for him, it's probably a good paradigm.

Only, it never felt so *hard* to avoid dating in my friend group before.

It'll be fine again, I'm sure, once Barbara starts dating someone new.

That stupid Davis guy from the party comes to mind. He's not terrible, I guess, but why does Barbara always date these lackluster guys? Are the decent guys too afraid to ask her out? The super-guys need to stop being weenies and just do it.

Barbara still hasn't replied when it's time to leave for my date. I really ought to be picking her up, I think, but Barbara arranged for me to meet Lila there.

At a taco stand.

This thing is going to crash and burn. I can feel it.

Whenever I want their tacos, I valet at the fancy place next door. Parking in NYC is a nightmare, so I valet whenever possible, and I pray they don't jack up my car. This time, I'm guessing they won't. Barbara's mom's Buick isn't nearly as bad as she said it was. And instead of the mothballs she joked about, it smells like cinnamon.

My grandma used to always carry around Big Red gum, and it smells just like that.

I kind of like it, really. It's almost Christmassy.

I'm finally getting out of the car and surrendering the keys when my phone buzzes. I whip it out, already smiling in anticipation of what Barbara might say about the pile of clothes. . .that she might have been worried was actually a photo of me, naked.

But it's not her.

Lila the Librarian says, *I'm here*.

Goodie.

I should be more excited. I'm doing what Dave told me to do, and what Barbara also thinks is the right move. And who knows? I've met dozens of air-brushed Lilas and never clicked before, but it only takes once, right?

I square my shoulders, and I walk into the taco stand. I'm prepared that she may look nothing like her photo. She may be a man. She may talk like my dad. Or maybe she'll hate books and say she thought it was a funny joke.

Only, when I see her, she looks exactly like her photo. She actually might be a little more luminescent in person.

"Lila?"

She smiles, and I notice her teeth are almost annoy-ingly perfect. That's a good thing, right?

"I'm Bentley. I hope you didn't wait long."

"I just got here." She stands and holds out her hand, like we're here for a business deal. Which is better than, like, biting her lip and blowing me a kiss or something, I guess.

I shake her hand, which is firm but not overpowering. If I were thinking of acquiring her business, that would be good.

"So you're a librarian," I say.

"That's what the paycheck says." She perches on the stool again.

"What other things does the paycheck say to you?"

She laughs. "Usually things like, 'sorry I'm not bigger.'"

"I don't imagine librarians are handsomely paid, not with our government being the employer."

"No, most people aren't all about raising taxes for that sort of thing."

The waiter comes, and she orders as fast as I do, which is nice.

"But, I do love what I do, and I decided when I was in high school that if I was going to work, it should be doing something I love."

The conversation's pretty fluid, and some of what she says is actually funny. Our tacos have finally arrived —she got three instead of just one like the last girl I brought here, which is refreshing—when my phone buzzes.

She's mid-sentence, but I can't help myself.

I whip it out.

"Is anything wrong?"

MY PHONE DIED.

That's it? One text?

Then another comes through. THEN I ALMOST DIED. BENTLEY, WHAT WERE YOU THINKING? I DELETED THAT LAST PHOTO BEFORE IT COULD LOAD.

I knew she had crappy internet, but that makes the joke way less funny. Actually, she kind of sounds mad.

"Is that work?" Lila's not being irritating. I just kind of quit paying attention without any warning. It's all my fault, but I'm still annoyed that she's prying.

"Oh." What do I say? "It is, yeah. It's someone who works for me." There. That's true.

My fingers fly over the letters. YOU'RE THE ONE BEING SILLY. THIS IS THE PHOTO I SENT. LET IT LOAD THIS TIME, YOU BIG PRUDE.

"You must like your job, too," Lila says.

"Huh?" I look up.

"You're smiling so big while you reply to a work text." She wipes her mouth with a napkin. "That's how I feel when I'm recommending my favorite authors to people, especially kids."

"Do you really like books that much?"

"People who read are just. . .they have more insight than other people. They've spent a lot of time looking through windows to other worlds and points of view, and it expands their minds."

My phone buzzes again, and like a junkie, I pick it up. PLEASE TELL ME YOU'RE NOT TEXTING ME ON YOUR DATE RIGHT NOW.

Not even a laugh? C'mon. IT'S YOUR FAULT. YOU TEXTED ME FIRST, AND IGNORING FRIENDS IS RUDE.

BENTLEY, DO NOT BLOW THIS. LILA'S THE MOST PROMISING OF THE THREE.

RELAX. I'M NOT BLOWING ANYTHING. I CAN TEXT YOU A PHOTO, AND THEN MAYBE YOU'LL BELIEVE ME.

DO NOT DO THAT.

WHY NOT? SHE LOOKS JUST LIKE HER PROFILE. YOU DID GREAT.

But when I look up, Lila's gone. She's written a note on a napkin. It says, "When you find a girl who makes you smile like those texts on your phone, don't let her slip away. -L"

Well, shoot.

But I did learn one important thing.

I had way more fun at that holiday party than I did getting tacos, even though Lila wasn't a man who was catfishing me. Now I just need to figure out whether it was the party setting or the person I went with. I have a pretty good suspicion that I already know the answer.

And Lila the Librarian already told me what to do.

But the girl I like thinks I'm a player, and the only reason we're hanging out and texting is so she can help me find someone else to date. So what do I do when the person I want to be with is only around to help me do something I no longer want to do?

I think about that all the way home, while I breathe in cinnamon and try to figure out what else to text. And if I scroll through the photos I took under the pretense of helping her see herself more clearly before I go to bed, well.

It's not like she doesn't know I took them.

9

BARBARA

When every other marketing and public relations firm was focused on mega-influencers, I was one of the first to insist on a micro-influencer branch. Even taking into account the amount of time involved in reaching out to twenty or thirty times as many influencers, it's more cost effective for our clients to pay a dozen small TikTokers with far better engagement and niched audiences than it is to land a few huge ones.

But that ignores the most important part of finding and focusing on micro-influencers.

When chosen properly, they will grow as the client grows, and that synergy can often springboard both of them at the same time, improving the reach and power of both. That's how I found Twinning, and I also recently discovered a brand that I think will be a *perfect fit* for them.

The gum's called Chump Change, and they offer a lot of the shreds packages, like old-school baseball packs used to have. It has a double letter in the first name, and they've been using a lot of old, classic ads, but changing them slightly, to push their old-school revival brand of gum.

It plays well to the kids who want the gum, as well as the parents who would be the ones buying it. Their target demographic is sports-playing kids at games and events. And the #Twinning girls play doubles tennis at school. I think a remake of something similar to the Double Double your enjoyment ad from DoubleMint would be a real #homerun.

Without realizing we're dealing with paperwork hangups, my marketing team already pitched the idea to Chump Change, and they're chomping at the bit to start laying down some plans. In fact, their boss, Gary French, has sent me an email *and* left me a voicemail asking when he can meet with them and telling me he'd like them to be the spearhead of their upcoming marketing campaign, and wanting to know if they'd be willing to do a commercial as well. He wants it all to go live on January one, and in marketing timelines, that means we're already four months behind.

I've been slammed on all fronts lately, especially as holiday plans are being implemented and adjusted, but it's time for me to make that home visit and figure out what the hangup is with their mother. It's a real fluke that they live right around the corner, really. Less than ten percent of our accounts live within a reasonable driving distance.

I plan to go in the morning, when hopefully their mother will be home and not busy with kid stuff. But by the time I put out all the fires that pop up, including all the necessary last-minute planning for the holiday party we have tonight—it's for a small but lucrative client and the CEO insisted on doing it at his personal residence, with us taking point—it's already late.

I whip out my phone to text Bentley. My heart races a little bit just thinking about him, and I hate to do this, but I do not have time to rush to his place to pick him up, and I can't expect him to drive forty minutes to this guy's home on the edge of the North End.

SLAMMED AT WORK. I'M SURE YOU ARE TOO. YOU CAN SKIP TONIGHT'S PARTY. IT'S NORTH OF THE CITY, AND IT'S AT SOME GUY'S HOUSE.

NICE TRY. I'M COMING.

Now my heart's really pounding. Shouldn't he be relieved to be off the hook? I CAN'T COME PICK YOU UP. I HAVE TO GO TO DEAL WITH AN ADMIN HURDLE AND THEN GO STRAIGHT THERE. And I'll be wearing my boring black suit, blue blouse, and slate heels.

Today is just not my day.

TEXT ME THE ADDRESS.

I should argue further. I should refuse to give him the info, but I did my part. I gave him an out, and if he doesn't want to take it, that's not on me. Right?

Right.

I can't help smiling on my way to the apartment listed on the twins' paperwork from last year. I hope they haven't moved. That would make this even more irritating. I got the distinct impression that money was really tight for the mom and that the girls' extra income really helped. You'd think she'd be a little more motivated to respond to my messages instead of letting her eleven-year-old daughters handle them.

When I get there, the mailbox still says McKinnon. That's promising.

I buzz the apartment, but no one answers. Luckily,

a neighbor waves me over. "They never answer for anyone but delivery," he says.

"They work for me, actually, so I swear I'm not up to anything nefarious," I say.

"Eh, you don't look too scary." He just bobs his head and ducks into his apartment after letting me through.

It was great he allowed me in, but it doesn't inspire confidence that they'll just wave anyone along.

I stumble down the line of apartments, many with numbers hanging askew, kick aside piles of accumulated leaves, and try to make sense of the bizarrely ordered rows. I do finally find theirs, and I tap on the door. It's four in the afternoon, so hopefully their mom's not picking them up from school or tennis practice or anything.

No one answers.

I bang.

Still nothing.

I'm about to give up and try to come back later, when I hear voices inside. Not loud ones, but it's enough that I know someone is home.

"Girls? It's me, Barbara from Follow. I just need to get some forms signed by your mom, and it'll be super quick. I have a new job for you, and it's a great one."

There's some scuffling around, and then a bit of whispering, and then the door opens a crack. "Barbara?" It's Nikki, I think. She has eyes that are slightly darker blue than Ricki's and her hair's almost always down, falling across her eyes.

"See?" I wave.

But she doesn't open the door. She just sticks her arm through the crack.

"The thing is, hon, I need to get your mom's signature. You two are minors, so I kind of need to confirm with her that it's fine for you to be working with us."

"Oh." She nods. "Well, I'll run it back to her, and then I'll bring it up to you. Will that work?"

It's strange. Why wouldn't her mother come to the door? "Is she not feeling well?" In that moment, I catch a whiff of something ripe from the inside of their apartment—like spoiled fruit or unwashed... something. It's not confidence-inspiring either.

Nikki looks worried. "She has a stomach ache."

"That's no good," I say. "Is there something I can do? I could run grab medicine, or I could take her to the doctor if that would help. I have a car."

Nikki shakes her head. "No, it's fine. She just can't come to the door."

I don't like it, but I finally pass the paper to her and wait.

Two minutes later, she's back, and the signature looks just like the one from before—like an eleven-year-old authored it.

Something is definitely up.

"Girls." I frown. "Is your mom really in there? Because I have a fiduciary duty to you and your mother to make sure that she knows what's happening."

"She's here. That's her signature." Nikki nods.

I know it's not. I pulled the paperwork and her signature did not look like that last year, but arguing with an eleven-year-old is like complaining that concrete's hardening. Useless. "Well, thanks."

I walk to the front of the complex and call my boss. "Are you almost here?" Jennifer usually avoids holiday parties like the plague—she's atheist and she hates pretending to celebrate Christmas. But Gary's a big enough client that she was stuck when he asked for her specifically.

"I've hit a small snag." I explain that I'm pretty sure the girls are forging their mom's signature and that I'm worried she may be sick or in trouble.

"You're not their babysitter," she says. "Put the paper in the file and as long as they're making their posts, don't worry about it. Are you worried they won't honor their obligations to the clients?"

"I mean, not exactly."

"Then what's the issue?"

"I'm worried about them," I say. "They're kids, and honestly, it kind of looks like their mom has either checked out or is in trouble."

"That sounds like their dad's issue."

"I've never heard anything about their dad," I say. "I think they had an affidavit on file saying they had only one guardian."

"Listen, you're not a judge and you're not a social worker, you're a marketer. You're *my* marketer, and I just found out they're doing holiday karaoke, so you're going to get your cute tushy over here in the next thirty minutes or else, because I can't sing, but I know you can." She hangs up.

Well.

I sigh long and slow, but when I start for my car, I feel really, really uncomfortable. Instead of heading to the party like I know I should, I call Seren and tell her the same thing I just told Jennifer.

"You know, life has a lot of paths."

"What are you talking about?" I ask.

"Only you know which one to take."

"Seren, I'm asking what I should do right now. I don't have time for some philosophical debate."

"You have a job," she says. "And tonight, you have a party to get to, right?"

"I do," I say. "Yes. I should go."

"But you didn't go. You called me instead."

"Only because. . ." I realize it sounds kind of dumb to say that I called her because she's a foster mom, and her kids are messed up, and I'm beginning to worry that these kids are messed up too.

"In my experience, people usually already know what they ought to do when they call to ask for advice," Seren says. "I can't tell you what the right move is, but your heart already knows, or you'd be in your car *en route* to that party."

I think about those sweet little girls, and I just *can't* go anywhere until I'm sure that they're alright.

"Can you send me your social worker's information?"

"Sure," Seren says. "But be warned. Alice is. . .a lot."

"That's fine," I say.

Only, I'm not expecting her to be quite so brusque. You'd think that social workers would be the first in line to try and help a child. "You have no evidence that these kids need a single thing," she says. "You have guesses and supposition. Their mom could have the flu. She could be working two jobs. She's replying to emails, they have an apartment to live in—unless you have more evidence than that, we have no right to even investigate. I can't document that we have a *hunch* there's something wrong, or that they *allegedly* forged a signature. I'd need to investigate half the kids at every school in America if that was enough."

"But—"

"If you find out something concrete, or if there's any real cause for you to think these kids aren't safe, call me back, but not before then."

Evidence? She wants evidence? Fine.

My next call is to Bentley. "I have a weird favor to ask."

"Stranger than pretending to be your boyfriend or swapping cars so I look like a regular guy?"

That makes me laugh. "Maybe." I explain what I want him to do, and after he agrees and reroutes to meet me here, I do a little research. By the time he gets here, I'm ready. I hand him a box that's actually still hot.

"Pizza?"

"This place is the closest pizza parlor to their apartment, and I'm guessing they've ordered from it before. Probably regularly." At least, the guy said they only open for delivery, and pizza is like delivery 101. Especially for little kids.

"Okay."

"So you need to tell them that they won the pizza, and then when they open the door, walk right on in to deliver it to their table."

"And you're going to follow me, say *Boo*, and take a look around?"

"You're making it sound creepy," I say. "I'm going to just peek in and see if their mother is anywhere to be found."

"And if she's not?" He arches one eyebrow.

"Then I'm going to ruin Alice's night."

"Who's Alice?"

"The social worker who thinks I'm crazy."

He nods. "So we have all the players assembled. The two kids, the marketing busybody, the social worker who thinks you're crazy, and your friend who also thinks you're crazy, but who's too afraid of you to say no."

I shove his shoulder.

"Just promise me one thing," he says.

"What?"

"I'm not going to be in jail at the end of the night, right?"

I roll my eyes. "Just go. It's that one on the end." I point. He looks back at me twice, but on the third time, I wave him forward and toss my head. "Go already."

He knocks lightly.

"Hello?" I can barely hear them from where I'm standing, two doors down.

"Pizza delivery."

"We didn't order pizza," one of them says.

"You won this one—it's a large half pepperoni, half cheese. It's our most popular pie."

"How did we win? We didn't enter a contest."

"It's a customer appreciation award," he says. "We chose randomly from our best customers over the past year."

"Oh." There's some kind of back and forth, but then I hear it.

The sound of a lock sliding in the door, and the grinding and groaning of the door being opened.

Exactly as I asked, Bentley shoves his way through.

"Hey," Nikki says. "Why's a pizza guy wearing a suit?"

"They made me," he says. "It's part of the award."

"You have to wear a suit?" Ricki shakes her head. "Just hand it to me."

"Look, I have to get a photo," he says. "With you holding the pizza. Do you want it or not?" He pauses like he doesn't care.

He's pretty good at this, if I'm being honest. I'm not sure I'd have come up with that. He hands the pizza to Nikki, and waves for Ricki to come over.

I whip out my phone, realizing what he's doing. He's getting me my evidence. As I come around the corner, the open door coming into view, I nearly freeze in place.

Their apartment would make a landfill look nice.

There's so much trash that I can't see a clear surface. Pizza boxes. Delivery cartons. Bags. Discarded and half-eaten food. I snap a few photos, and then I move closer.

"Hey," Nikki says. "Why are you still here?"

"Actually." Bentley turns around. "She's with me."

Ricki—I think, since her hair is in a ponytail—scowls. "I knew it. I told you we didn't win any contest."

"Girls." When I step inside the room, the smell's overpowering. I'm not sure how it didn't slap me in the face when they cracked the door earlier. "Is your mother really here?"

Looking around at the trash, and holding as steady as I can when a cockroach runs across the pile right in front of me, I'm virtually certain there are no adults present.

"Is she at the hospital?" Bentley asks.

"She was." Ricki's eyes flash. "Before."

"Before what?" I almost don't want to know.

"She died three months ago," Nikki says. "But we've been living here alone for almost a year, and we're fine."

"Where's your dad?" Bentley asks.

"Who knows?" Ricki asks. "And who cares?"

"You can't live here alone," I say. "It's not safe."

"Yeah, creeps could pretend we won a prize and break in." Ricki tosses the box on the sofa and folds her arms, glaring.

"Touché," I say. "But I did that because I was worried about you."

"Well, you don't need to worry," she says. "We have

more money than ever now that we don't have to pay the medical bills."

I hate that I left my phone on, videotaping what she said, but it's the evidence Alice will need, I imagine. I text it to her—photos, the video.

"Girls, I've been talking to a social worker, and—"

"No." Nikki picks up the pizza box and throws it at the door. "Get out. We don't want anyone to 'help' us." She makes air quotes.

"They have systems in place for this," I say. "The help is real."

"Our friend Madison went to an orphanage and she said it's horrible," Nikki says.

"She probably went to a group home," I say. "They don't really have orphanages anymore."

"Who cares what they call it?" Ricki asks. "We can pay our rent, and we are. We usually go to school, too. So leave us alone."

"How about we work on trying to get this place cleaned up," I say. "Because the social worker will be here soon, and I imagine it'll look better if it's not totally full of trash." When I grab a half-full bag from the corner, a rat explodes out of it, leaping toward my face.

He pivots and hops over my shoulder, his poky little claws racing down across my back as he books it for the door. I was unprepared, though, and I definitely scream.

Really long, and really loud.

"The rats leave you alone," Nikki says. "Unless you try to clean."

I can't help shuddering. "You cannot stay here tonight."

"Where do you think we're going, then?" Ricki

asks. "Because we're not going to a group home." She folds her arms and sets her jaw.

"What if they let you come stay with me?" I ask.

They don't say no, but they don't look excited, either. I'm probably not their favorite person right now, and that's okay.

"What about him?" Nikki glares at Bentley. "I'm guessing he's not really a pizza guy."

"He's not," Bentley says. "*He's* a friend of Barbara's."

"I asked him to help, because the neighbor told me you only let delivery people through the door."

The girls keep arguing with me, and Bentley braves his way through filling and taking out as many bags and boxes of trash as they have in the apartment before Alice arrives. He dislodges three more rats, but one of them is pretty small.

Impressively, he never shrieks. He doesn't even whimper, not even when the bottom falls out of a soggy box and covers his fancy shoes in sludge. The smell gets worse, which surprises me, but maybe that's normal in a clean-up operation.

When Alice gets there, I think the place is looking way better, but she still looks horrified. I task Bentley to keep the girls busy so we can talk with a tiny bit of privacy in the front entry area. "I've called the central office for an emergency placement, and I think—"

"What about me?" I ask.

"You have to have a home study and take classes on fostering—"

"I have," I say. "And so has he." I toss my head at Bentley.

"Right," Alice says. "Because you're friends with Seren and Dave."

"I'm Seren's family now," I say. "So of course I had to

go through all the training and approvals so I'd be an option for respite care. Their youngest is a teenager at this point, but I revised my home study after my divorce in case they ever had to leave the country. Plus, with them, you never know when they'll take someone else in."

Alice smiles. "Or, apparently, when you will."

"Girls," I say, moving back into the main part of the apartment. "Let's get your bags packed. I have a really nice guest room."

"Do you actually have a deluxe guest room?" Bentley asks.

I shrug. "Deluxe might be a stretch, but compared to this place, it's the Ritz frigging Carlton."

He laughs. "I'm assuming it's cockroach and rodent free."

"Last I checked," I say. "Doing the dishes every day really helps me."

"I haven't seen that many rats in years," he says. "And I visit the City pretty often."

I drop my voice to a whisper while Alice is interrogating the girls. "You think I'm crazy for bringing them to my place?"

"I'm not the one you should worry about." He looks pointedly at my phone where it's poking out of my purse. It's lit up again—Jennifer has called at least eight times.

"I have a party I need to go by," I say. "Is there any chance I could do that and *then* take them home?"

Alice had picked up a call, which I didn't realize. She says, "Lemme call you right back."

"Sorry," I say. "It's just that—"

"You should let me place them with a foster home that's ready for this kind of thing." She frowns. "I pulled your file, and you're recently divorced."

It feels like she just slapped me. "Does that really matter?"

"Divorce wrecks people, and being a foster parent wrecks people, and in my experience, most people who are already recovering from something aren't ready for the fallout."

"I'm ready," I say. "It's fine. I don't have to go to the party."

She arches her eyebrow. "Are you sure?"

I nod.

"Will skipping this party get you fired?" She compresses her lips into a flat line. "Because I don't want to stick these girls with you and have to move them elsewhere inside of seventy-two hours because your boss is threatening to fire you for caring for them properly."

I shake my head. "It'll be fine."

"The first three days are going to be the hardest on all of you."

Nikki's just coming out of her room, a massive backpack that looks dramatically overloaded on her back, and a huge duffel bag dragging across the floor behind her.

I cannot think about what she's dragging it through, or what may have hitched a ride in the bags.

I've watched the news for thirty years of my life, and I've seen a lot of clips of prisoners of war being brought home. Nikki's eyes look like that—like she's wary and tired and angry and scared.

I found them. I care about them. After spending time with Dave and Seren, I have an inkling of what's in store for me. I firmly believe I'm their best placement. That matters more than a job I don't even love.

"They can come with me."

Alice stares at me without saying a word for ten

seconds. Then for twenty. Finally, around the very awkward thirty seconds mark, she nods. "Alright. But you will call me if you find that you can't do this, and you will not let those girls suffer through more trauma on your watch."

"I won't," I say.

"You think I'm being hard on you, but those girls have no other advocate."

In that moment, I realize that Alice is so gruff because her heart's constantly flayed wide open. I'm not sure I could survive handling a job like hers. Being called at all hours to remove kids from their homes, like tearing feral kittens out of their dens underneath someone's warehouse. Then she has to pass them off to someone else, knowing that she won't be able to do much if they're not properly cared for other than ripping them away yet again.

There are too many injured, neglected feral kittens in this world. Alice can't care for them all. Neither can I. But I found these two, and I can care for them. So I will.

"Alright," I say. "Nikki, Ricki, let's go. Anything you forgot, we can come back for tomorrow. Don't stress."

"Rent's only paid through Wednesday of next week," Ricki says. "Can we come back before then?"

I pity the landlord, having this bomb dropped on him or her next week. "Absolutely," I say. "We will."

"I'll come and help," Bentley says. "In fact, if you need—"

I shake my head. "You've been a huge support, but I'll get them home from here."

"Are you sure?" He studies my face carefully.

I nod. "I'll call you tomorrow."

Ironically, once we're out of the apartment complex and moving, like stray kittens might, both of them fall asleep in the car on the way to my place. And when we get there, neither of them says a word. They drag their bags inside, refuse to shower or bathe, and fall asleep on the queen bed in my guest room, curled up into two little balls.

I almost feel guilty about thinking of them as stray cats, because they're so similar. I want to go to sleep as well, but instead, I do the very thing I'd rather avoid.

I call my boss.

She picks up halfway through the first ring. "I should fire you," she says.

"The girls' mom died three months ago, and they've been living alone for almost a year while paying her medical bills and their own living expenses."

She's utterly silent on the other end.

"They're at my house now—I'm their emergency foster placement, and they'll be staying with me for a while."

"Barbara."

I'd feel bad too, if I were her. "It's going to be fine," I say. "But they may need a little bit of extra attention for the next little while. I'll still be at work, of course, but after they get out of school, I may need to leave a bit early."

"Barbara," Jennifer says, "I told you to get in the car and come to the party."

"I know," I say. "But I knew there was something wrong, and I was right about that."

"And now it's your problem, because you doggedly insisted on *making it* your problem. And that means that now it's also my problem, and I don't like having more problems. I'm not even sure whether they can be our client, with you as their temporary guardian. Have you thought of that?"

"Wait." I can't believe this. "Are you upset that I helped them?"

"You're shocked by that? You ignored me, and then you did exactly what I said not to do, and then you didn't show for a party we were in charge of handling—leaving me holding the very empty, very disorganized bag. I looked like an idiot tonight, because you insisted on becoming a white knight."

"You had James and Kristy with you, and I had already lined everything up. The food, the decorations, the band, and even the cake were already there. I went by earlier to make sure—"

"I had to introduce Gary and the rest of the management team, and I had to give your speech, and I had no idea that any of that was going to fall to me. I looked basically incompetent, which I hate more than anything else."

"Did you hear any of what I said?" I wish I could slap her through the phone receiver. "Two little girls' mother is *dead* and they have no one to care for them. They were living in squalor, surrounded by rats and roaches, and no one even *knew*."

"Two little girls I've never met, and to whom you had zero obligation were struggling," Jennifer says. "The reality is that the world is full of sob stories, but we can't be expected to do something about all of them, and—"

"I'm going to pretend you didn't just say any of that to me," I say. "I'm going to tell myself that you're really drunk or something, and that you aren't being yourself. Because if I really thought you felt that way, if I really thought you were so selfish that you would order me to walk away from those little girls when I knew something was majorly off, then you wouldn't have to fire me, Jennifer. I'd quit and never look back, and then tonight would be the first in a long line of holiday parties this season that you'd be handling. All. By. Yourself."

I hang up.

Before I collapse in bed, which I badly want to do, I call Seren, and the second she answers, I start to cry. "I have no idea how you did this for so many years," I say. "I'm scared, and I'm exhausted, and I might get fired, and I have no idea what I'll do if that happens."

Seren spends more than thirty minutes talking to me, and even though I'm tired, I feel way, way better when we're finally done. "I'll come over and watch them any time you need me to over the next few weeks," Seren says.

"I can't ask you to do that. You have the inn, and Dave and Killian, and with the holidays—"

"You watched the kids how many times for me?" Seren asks. "Countless. Whenever I felt like I was at the end of my rope, you came running. I can help you now, and I'm happy to do just that."

"I'm just not sure why I did it. My boss thinks I'm insane, and even though I got mad at her, now I'm wondering whether she's right."

"You're not insane. I know how you felt—I felt the same way when I met Emerson. You just lost your mom, and now you see these poor girls who lost their mother in an even worse way."

In that moment, I realize that Seren's a genius.

I lost my mom a little more than a year and a half ago now, and then I lost my dad shortly after. Then my husband quit on me, and I've never really felt more alone than I have this year.

But when I saw those girls, I realized how lucky I have been. I had my mom when it mattered. I had her for all the years that I was in school, when I couldn't care for myself. Now that she's gone, I have a job, a career, a support system of friends, and I can drive myself to and from things. I had a father and a mother who both loved me and they kept me safe for a really long time.

No matter how alone I feel, my mom taught me to be self-sufficient. These girls have no one—and they can't do anything for themselves. So Jennifer may think I'm insane, and maybe she's even right, but now those helpless girls have me for as long as they need me. Through my tears, I manage to squeeze out a "Thank you" for Seren.

"Your parents may be gone, but you have a lot of family who loves you," Seren says. "Don't ever forget that, and reach out to me whenever you need it. Phone call. Babysitter. Grocery delivery. Pedicure date. What-ever. Okay?"

It feels like calling Seren's helping me realize a lot of things I should already have known. "I barely know them," I say. "But I don't want to give these girls up."

"I know," she says. "I knew that when you called me earlier."

Of course she did. Seren's an emotional genius. "Unless you think they could find a better place to live."

"I think people come into our lives for a reason," she says. "I've always thought that, but anyone who has met you and heard about how you found them would agree. Alice already told me she thinks those girls went *home* tonight."

After bawling for another half hour, I finally go to sleep.

10

BENTLEY

In first grade, my parents had me tested, and they found that I had an IQ far above the average. They put me in gifted classes, and I had special tutors. They did everything they could to make sure I had every opportunity to excel.

By the time I was thirty, I'd started my own business.

By the time I was thirty-five, my business was a raging success.

I've proven that test right over and over and over. But I also do my share of stupid things. Even so, one of the dumbest things I've ever done was give Barbara my eHarmony login.

"I told you," she's saying over the phone. "The date with Lila the Librarian may have been a bust, but that doesn't mean—"

"She *disappeared* in the middle of our meal, Barbara." I don't tell her why or how I failed to notice until she was gone.

"Okay, so it was a bust. That's fine. More often than not, even when you play the odds, you don't get a love connection on the first try, but you know numbers better than I do. What are your chances of finding Mrs. Right when you never go on dates at all?"

I roll my eyes, but it's totally wasted. She can't even see me. "We should have done a video chat," I say.

"I'm on the road," she says. "I just dropped the girls off at school, remember?"

"Listen, it's not a good time for you right now, so let's just table the dating thing until after Christmas."

"Why does it need to be a good time for *me?*" I can practically hear her rolling her eyes through the phone, so maybe she could tell earlier when I did it.

"Because." Like stepping on a Lego, the answer shoots through me. "I'm not going on another date unless you're there to analyze it." Then I tell a brilliant, gifted lie. "I have no idea why she left, so I could just do the same thing wrong I did that time again and again."

"Bentley, I do not have the bandwidth to go on any dates right now."

Which is exactly why I want to push pause and wait until you are. "That's why I said we should wait," I say. "We can do this in the new year, no problem."

"You need to do this while you have the excitement to try it." It sounds like she's parking and getting out. That means I'm quickly running out of talk time.

"I'll still be excited after Christmas."

"I won't, even then," she says. "I'm not sure when I'll want to double, so you should—"

"Wait, who said anything about double dating?" I ask.

"Huh?" She sounds nervous now.

"You could just come along, sit at the table behind me, and listen."

"Like some kind of super-stalker?" She scoffs.

"Bentley, you have got to be kidding me. If I'm sitting there during your date, she'll recognize me when we meet."

"You're assuming things will go well enough that I'd bring her to family functions later," I say.

"You should be assuming that too!"

I guess she's right, with the information she has available. "Okay, fine. You can sit two tables over, and I'll only ask you to do it for our first date. I'll make sure that you're only in *my* line of sight."

She sighs. "I'm at work, Bentley."

"No problem," I say.

"I set up your date for today already." I can hear the giddiness in her voice, dropping that on me now, like a sneak attack.

"You're kidding."

"Not at all," she says. "It's just a lunch date, so it's low pressure. It's the not-bomb-girl you weren't keen on, but you never know. Give it a chance. She said she's fine with eating anywhere, so I picked that cafe by your office. They have a pretty good turkey melt."

"And you'll be there to eat one too, right?"

She huffs. "Bentley."

"Did I mention that I called your boss and told her that I would be moving my marketing to your firm, but only if you handled it?"

"You don't even need marketing."

"Three of my clients do," I say. "And I called them and told them you're the best."

"Of all the—Bentley!"

"Be there at lunch. Please?"

She grumbles like crazy, and clearly she's climbing up the stairs to her building entrance, but right as she hangs up, she says, "Fine."

After I'm virtually certain she's going to be in a

meeting or otherwise occupied, I open the app, dig around and find the message with this Oppenheimer person, and I tell her I can't make it today. I'm subjected to an obscene number of emojis, but she finally agrees that we can postpone.

My assistant at work has to help me, but I manage to delete everything after the message I sent saying where to meet. That should keep Barbara from realizing the date was called off by me.

I can't help my evil smile.

"Is this the lady you helped last night?" Oliver asks.

"Yep," I say.

"The one who's now fostering two little girls?" He looks like he's asking whether she has a horrible case of athlete's foot.

"Yes, that's Barbara."

"And you're wanting to meet her there, while this woman—the cute, smiley one—is going to supposedly stand you up. Right?"

I nod.

Oliver scratches his face scruff. "I do not understand what you're doing at all."

I ought to be angry. I mean, he's basically saying I'm stupid for wanting to date Barbara. I whip out my phone and pull up a photo of Barbara—my favorite one. She's half-smiling at the woman from that makeup company, and she's clearly in her element.

"Now you'll get it." I swivel it around.

"You know I'm gay, right?" Oliver pulls a face.

"You can still recognize beauty." I shake the phone.

"I can," Oliver says, "and that woman on the app is objectively way prettier. And she's not chubby."

"You're an idiot," I say. "And you're wrong. Barbara looks amazing."

"They do say it's in the eye of the beholder," he mutters as he walks off.

"I can fire you, you know, and I will if you make one more comment about Barbara not being good enough."

"You didn't fire me when I accidentally booked you to Macedonia when you were supposed to go to Malaysia."

"This is a bigger deal than botched travel plans," I say. "Watch what you say."

"Barbara does have good taste in fashion. For someone who's clearly on a budget."

It's not glowing, but it's something. Oliver's always a little brutal in his honesty, but he never makes up compliments.

"You're moving in the right direction at least," I concede.

Oliver reminds me half an hour before my lunch that it's almost time, so I wrap up my client call. "You're redeeming yourself."

"Don't blurt anything out," Oliver says as I'm leaving.

"What?"

"You're a straightforward guy," he says. "It's usually good. No messing around. But if this woman just got divorced—"

"It's been almost seven months," I say.

"*Just* got divorced," Oliver says, his eyes wide and his tone patronizing, "and if she's opened her home to two little girls, she may be. . .overwhelmed. It may not be the right time for you to spring anything heavy on her."

Well, shoot.

Is he right? Am I being selfish, wanting to date her now?

I'm not in a great mood when I walk into the cafe,

at least, not until I see her sitting in the corner booth. I can't help my smile, and I lift my hand to wave.

She scowls at me and shakes her head. Then she pointedly looks at the door. Because she has no idea that Oppenwhatever isn't coming. Maybe I'm not so smart.

After ten minutes of her ignoring me, I start to get frustrated. I'm definitely not going to get anywhere with her if we can't even talk on our fake date. And with the cutest little girls in the world at her place, it's not like I can ask her out for night things.

"How late is she?" I stage-whisper.

Barbara glances at her watch, her hair falling forward to block her face. "Almost twenty minutes. We should check and see if she's messaged something."

Now I'm alarmed. What if *Barbara* sends her a message, and she replies saying that *I* cancelled? "I don't want to seem clingy."

She frowns. "But she should have at least warned you if she was running late."

I stand up and slide into Barbara's booth.

"Whoa." She shoos me back. "What are you doing?"

"You've been eating," I say. "But I'm starving." I steal a bite of her turkey melt. "Oh, you weren't kidding. That is good."

She snatches it away. "That's mine." But when our hands meet, a spike of energy shoots through me.

Forget the sandwich—I want to grab her hand again. But I need an excuse. "I have another meeting soon." I reach my arm around her shoulders and try to snake the rest of that sandwich half. "I'm paying anyway. C'mon. You can share a little."

But when I do grab it, I'm a little disappointed.

Now I don't have an excuse to keep my arm around her. I didn't think this through.

"Just take it." She shakes my arm off and shifts as far inside the booth as she can.

Maybe Oliver's right. Maybe it's too much too fast.

The second bite of the sandwich isn't nearly as good as the first. Maybe it was touching her that really made it taste amazing. "Well, thanks."

"I was full anyway," she says. "Look how big their sandwiches are."

"How are the girls?"

She leans back with a sigh. "I want to keep them." I can tell that she's expecting me to be surprised.

"I know."

"What?" Now she stiffens, and then she narrows her eyes. "What do you mean, *you know?*"

"I could tell last night."

"I've never wanted to foster kids," she says.

"You haven't needed to. You've always helped Dave and Seren, but Killian's mostly grown."

"You say that like I'm a mother hen who needs chicks or something."

"Would that be a bad thing?" I can't help smiling. "There aren't enough mother hens in the world. But I'd describe you more like a mother lion, honestly."

She's smiling, now. "Really?"

"Absolutely," I say. "Last night—I've never seen you look more glorious." I pull out my phone. "Look." I swipe until I reach the photo of her on the phone with Alice, her arms waving wildly, her eyes fiery. "See?"

Lioness.

She can see it, too. I can tell. But when she turns toward me, her face looks strange. "Why'd you take this photo, Bentley?"

Ah, shoot. I didn't think that part through. "Um. I mean—"

"You don't have to keep sending me pictures to show me that I look good. It's a nice gesture, but it's not necessary."

Thank goodness. I made my own cover—I just forgot about it until she reminded me. As usual, Barbara's saving me from myself. Even on the date she doesn't know I only made so I could date her. "I think it is still necessary." I lean forward, resting my elbows on the table. "Unless you're saying that now you believe me?"

She rolls her eyes.

"Then I'll just have to keep taking and sending them."

"Would you like anything else?" The waitress has a pencil tucked behind her ear, and she's smiling at us. "Or was the rest of hers enough for you, big guy?"

She thinks we're a couple.

I love it.

"Oh, he's not my—"

I wrap my arm around her shoulders again. "I'm good," I say.

When the waitress leaves, Barbara shimmies until I move my arm again. "What was that?"

"I have to do a little practicing," I say. "When's the next holiday party?"

"I can't keep asking you to come to those," she says. "So far, these dates have all been a bust, which means I haven't helped you at all." She whips out her phone. "Speaking of, I'm about to rip her a new one. Thirty minutes, and nothing?" She's shaking her head.

"Wait." I put my hand on hers, and it happens again. That little zing. I close my fingers around hers slowly.

Her mouth drops open and her eyes widen and slowly, they rise to mine. "What?"

Right. I said to wait. "Don't bother," I say. "If she doesn't come back with some kind of great explanation?" I shrug. "Then we've learned that she's unreliable."

She frowns. "You're really zen about all this."

I shrug. "Oppenheimer never felt right to me. Plus, I feel like the right person is out there, and I just need to have the right timing." I stare right at her as I say it, but she seems to have no inkling that I'm talking about her.

Maybe Oliver's right. Maybe the timing is still wrong for us.

Well, I'm not in a rush. It's been fifteen years already. I can wait a few more months. Or even a year, if that's what it takes. I'm learning from Lucky what I should have already seen with Dave and Seren's kids. Lucky's still a bit of a mess, but she gets better day by day. Barbara may be struggling, but day by day, she's going to be closer and closer to ready, too.

Love, real love, takes time to be developed. And to grow.

"Alright, well, I'm sorry she didn't come." She glances at her watch yet again. "Thirty-five minutes?" She shakes her head. "I'm calling it."

"Do you have somewhere to go?"

"I need to go pick some things out for the girls. I want them to have some presents under the tree."

"Oh, like what?" I ask.

"I have no idea," she says. "But I don't even have a tree yet, so." She laughs.

"Neither do I," I say. "Maybe I'll tag along."

She blinks. "You said you have a meeting."

"Oh." I glance at my phone. "Oliver says they bumped it back."

I worry she might argue with me, or call me on having a fake meeting, but she doesn't.

She just bumps me with her hip to push me out of the booth. "Let's go, then."

Again, that bump is like the first bite of cotton candy. Like a quick dip on a roller coaster. And like those things, now that I've felt it, I need *more*.

"Where's the closest tree farm?" I ask as we walk out.

"I have no idea." Her lip's twitching. "I was just going to go over there." She points at the little stand set up in the park.

"Duh," I say. "But how will you get it home?"

"The benefit of having a crappy car is that you can strap a tree to the top of it no problem." She looks unbearably smug.

As we walk to the stand, I'm actually a little impressed. It's a kids' park in the middle of Scarsdale, but they've done a nice job dressing it up. There are a plethora of blinky lights roping off the area, and they have decorated trees on each of the four corners. To top it all off, "O Holy Night" is playing softly.

The Santa's Forest sign is beautiful, and they have several cute reindeer made of pine clippings and lights sprinkled around the area. It looks like they're for sale, and I'm gripped with an uncharacteristic desire to buy one.

I actually feel a little bad for not getting a tree myself over the past few years. "Do you always get a tree?" I think I want a tree and a reindeer and, well, *everything* this year, because I like all the feelings I'm having right now, and I want to keep them around any way I can.

"Mom and Dad always bought live trees. Last year, I just didn't have the heart for it, but. . ."

Because of the girls, she wants to bring back an old family tradition. It's got to be good for her. After picking the two nicest trees they have, I point at the sign. "Do I get a discount if I have you deliver *two?*"

The man smiles. "Five bucks off."

"I don't need mine delivered," Barbara says. "I have my car."

"Relax," I say, "and let me do things my way, for once."

"Do you two really need two trees?" he asks, a sly look on his face.

"For now we do," I say. "Next year? Who knows?" I can't help my wink.

And if it makes Barbara roll her eyes, well, I'm finding that I like riling her up.

"Throw in a few strings of lights," I say, "and we've got a deal."

"The lights are nine bucks a strand," he says.

"Of course they are," I say. "How many do you think we need? Three or four strands each?"

I pay for Barbara's tree and mine, and I destroy the savings from my half-hearted negotiations by way over-tipping him.

"I better get back," Barbara says. "I have to meet the guy with the delivery later, right after I pick up the girls."

"Do you need me to do that?"

"But you have a meeting." She definitely looks suspicious now. "Right?"

"I do," I say. "But it's a call. I can do it from anywhere."

"I'm fine," she says. "The girls have tennis after school, so the times work out."

"That's good if you're looking for stuff to get them for Christmas. Tennis requires lots of equipment and clothing, and with their little twin account, matching gear would be adorable."

"Hey, you're right. Good idea."

"If you need something between now and tomorrow night, let me know."

"I could set up another date for you tomorrow instead," she says. "I feel terrible that the first two were so lousy."

Because I ruined them both. . . "I'm actually looking forward to tomorrow's holiday party. We have some reparations to make for bailing on last night."

"I do," she says. "You don't owe me or my boss anything."

"Still. I'm happy to help."

"Bentley, seriously."

I grab her arm—I can't help it. Touching her is like sour cream and onion Pringles. "You were amazing last night. You're doing something incredibly hard that very few people would have done. I care about those little girls too now, and I want to help. Let me."

She frowns a bit, and then slowly, she nods. "I'm not great at taking help."

"I'm not sure you've ever been offered much."

She looks at her shoes.

"That's going to change," I whisper.

"What?"

I shake my head. "Nothing. I'm just saying, helping you make things right at work is the least I can do."

And being around her, helping her help those little girls, is the best feeling I've had in a long time. Instead of buying pine bough reindeer, I'm planning to keep the source of the joy at my side as long and as often as possible.

Decorating the Christmas tree was my single favorite thing to do every year around this time. Mom would put on holiday music, and she'd wear a Christmas sweater. Dad would splurge on fancy cheese and crackers, and he'd always wear this really ugly holiday sweatshirt with reindeer that had bells around their necks.

He always sounded like one of those bell-ringing Salvation Army guys, klonking around the house with boxes of lights.

It was my job to take the old, janky strands of lights and change out the broken ones for new lights to get them going. And then Dad and I would wrap the tree while Mom directed from ten feet away. After we got it suitably lit, Mom would pull out the box of decorations, and she'd remind me of the history of each one.

My first year in the family handprint.

My kindergarten apple. It was cracked, but I'd written my name on it—badly.

My graduation hat from high school.

The bizarre and lopsided stocking I had crocheted.

The hot glue holding the hook on it was always coming off, but Mom never complained.

I have the box sitting next to the mantel, and I've ordered a rush job on some stockings that will hopefully kind of match the one Mom knit for me. Would the girls think I'm crazy if I hung Mom and Dad's, too?

Only, we don't even get that far.

"I hate Christmas trees," Nikki says.

"I don't want it either," Ricki says.

It's my own fault for imagining how nice this evening was going to be. If I've learned anything from Dave and Seren, it's that expectations with foster kids are always a mistake.

"You hate the tree?" I ask. "Or the lights? Or. . ."

"All of it," Nikki says. "It's at the heart of what's wrong with Christmas."

What's wrong with Christmas? "Nothing is wrong with Christmas," I say without thinking.

"Are you serious?" Nikki holds out her hand and starts throwing up fingers. "The commercialization, the myth of lying to kids about some creepy fat man crawling into their houses, the greed, the two weeks off for one specific holiday that lots of other religions don't even celebrate."

"Or what about how they club you over the head with Christmas songs on the radio, Christmas themes in school, and people ringing bells asking you for money on every street corner?" Ricki looks just as upset as her twin.

"But—"

"Listen, it's her house," Nikki says. "She can do what she wants." She slings her backpack on the ground and ducks into my guestroom.

Ricki scowls at me as she follows her sister.

"Okay," I say, "but—"

The door slams, effectively shutting down my attempt to figure out *why* they're so mad. Are they really upset about how commercial it is? Or is it something else? I know from my foster training that anger's a masking emotion, but heck if I know what they're masking underneath all that regurgitated holiday hate.

The guy who delivered the poor unliked tree left it in a five-gallon bucket in the middle of my living room after sawing a huge chunk off the bottom to make sure it hadn't sealed over with sap. He gave me strict instructions to keep the bucket full for more than twenty-four hours before putting it in the pretty base I bought, or rather, that Bentley bought.

And now I'm staring at a perfectly shaped, slightly leaning tree in an orange bucket, next to a pile of brand new twinkle lights. As I refill the bucket—it's already drunk a surprising amount of water—I'm thinking about how this is *so* not the Christmas I had in mind when I took the girls in last night. I had, stupidly, thought that we might sing, open presents, drink cocoa, and gather around a roaring fire in the fireplace I never use.

I've never been Santa before.

But apparently I wasn't missing much. He's just a creepy, fat man who breaks-and-enters anyway. Geez. My hand is itching to call Seren, but I feel like if I call her now, I'll never be able to figure anything out on my own. So instead, I sit down at the table and try to think.

I know very little about the girls, except that their mother got cancer—pancreatic—and she was very sick for a while, and then she was just gone. The girls were afraid of where they'd go. Dad has never been involved. They say they can't even reach him. And after living alone—paying their bills from their relatively meager influencer checks—they were caught, by the very person paying those checks.

They must not like me much at a base line.

And they clearly don't trust me at all. Any trust we had evaporated when I shoved Bentley through their door with a pizza and summoned Alice to evict them from the only home they cared about. I sigh and collapse back against the hard wooden chair.

I'm not winning them over with my brilliant cooking or festive holiday spirit, either. I need to figure out whether they really hate Christmas, or whether they just hate me, and by extension, anything I suggest.

"Alright, girls. It's almost dinner time," I call. "How about Chinese food?"

"We hate Chinese," one of them says. "Too greasy."

"Yeah, we don't want to have a heart attack," the other says.

At some point, I'm hoping I can tell them apart more easily, and hopefully I'll know which is speaking without looking at their hairstyle or eye color. Probably something their real mom just knew innately.

But now they're stuck with remedial mom.

"Alright, what about Italian? We can go out or order in."

"We just had pizza last night."

That was definitely said with a sneer.

"Okay, maybe burgers?" If they hate this too, they're definitely turning down everything that comes from me.

"Fine."

Great. So which is it?

Are they really picky and they just got tired of turning every single thing down? Or do they plan to make every single thing hard now that I'm the one running the show?

And most importantly, how can I fix this?

"Wanna come out and help me pick a place?"

"Anything's fine."

That's clearly not true. "Two double cheeseburgers with fries?"

"Sure."

"Girls, can you please come out?"

The door opens, and they step out, Nikki first, and then Ricki. They line up in front of the door with smiles plastered on their faces.

"I know you're mad at me."

"We aren't upset. We're very grateful to you." Ricki's still smiling her terrifying faux-grin.

"Do you really hate Chinese?"

Nikki nods slowly, still smiling.

"And you aren't upset that I hauled you here, to my house?"

"It's a lovely apartment with way less rats." Nikki's smile slips a little, but I'm not making much progress. Maybe there's a reason people use bright lights and big buckets of water for their interrogations.

"Look, I know the last few days haven't been perfect, and I know I'm easy to be angry with."

"We're grateful, Mrs. McDougal. We really are." Only, Ricki doesn't sound at all grateful. She sounds like she's smiling like a robot and ignoring any attempt I make at a real interaction.

I'm sick of it. All of it. And I'm tired. This isn't what I had in mind for this week, either. "Actually, I'm not Mrs. McDougal anymore," I say, with more bitterness than I probably ought to use with two tiny girls. "After my parents passed away, I got pretty depressed, and I ate a lot. Then I got fat, as you can see, and my husband didn't love that. So he divorced me. I've gone back to my maiden name, Champion."

The smiles slide off the girls' faces.

"You can be mad at me, and that's alright. I can take it, but I might get a little frustrated too, from time to time." I sigh. "I'm sorry that I snapped. I promise that I'll be honest with you, no matter what, and I know it'll be hard, but I hope that someday, you can be a little more honest with me. I can't help you unless I know what you need, and I'll keep doing things wrong unless you tell me how to do them right."

Nikki's mouth wobbles and she sniffs. At least the China-doll smiles are gone.

"Your mom died?" Ricki's eyes have welled up with tears.

I nod. "I'm an old lady, so I know it's not the same, but last year, my mom suffered a stroke, and she didn't recover. She had another one a few days later, and she slipped into a coma."

Ricki rushes at me, and I'm worried she's going to hit me.

But she hugs me instead.

"Oh." Now I'm crying, too.

"I'm sorry." Nikki's kicking at the floor, at nothing on the floor, as far as I can tell. But when she glances up, she's crying too.

"It's alright," I say. "It still hurts, more some days than others, and you may see me crying sometimes, but it gets a little bit easier every week."

Ricki's holding me so tightly that I worry about the circulation in my legs a little.

"We do like Chinese food," Nikki says quietly. "And we like Italian, too."

"Maybe we can get Chinese tonight." Ricki finally releases me. "Beef and broccoli is my favorite, and Nikki likes orange chicken, as long as it's not too spicy."

"What about egg rolls?" I ask. "Because if you don't like sweet and sour sauce, I may have to rethink having you living here with me. You might be aliens in human suits."

They both laugh. And as we sit and eat Chinese food together, neither of them talk about the tree, or Christmas, or their mom, but they do smile. And they do talk about school a little, and they tell me about a tennis match where they destroyed the two girls who were supposed to win the whole tournament.

It's a start.

Which is better than the slamming door I faced earlier.

It's a little surprising to me that our start came after I snapped at them, but I think it's because I was real. Whatever else we feel as humans, we can sense true authenticity. We can tell when someone's being honest. It's hard for us not to respond to that, at least in some way.

So when Nikki and Ricki have finished their homework, and they have both showered, and they're ready for bed, I try to prepare them for tomorrow.

"I have a weird job," I say. "Especially around Christmas, it means I have to attend a lot of client parties."

"Oh." Nikki frowns. "I don't want to go."

"You don't have to," I say. "My best friend—you guys can call her Aunt if you want—Seren's coming over to be with you. She'll make dinner and dessert— she's an actual chef, so believe me when I say you're in for a treat."

"So you're going alone?" Ricki asks. "Doesn't your husband work with you?"

I wasn't sure whether she'd remember that. I cringe

a little. "He will be there, and he's not super nice to me."

"I hate him," Nikki says. "Maybe I can go. They can't get mad at a little kid for punching him in the nose, but I hit really hard."

"She hit someone with a racket once, and she broke their nose," Ricki says.

"It was an accident." Nikki looks nervous.

"No one needs to punch him," I say. "Although, the guy who's going with me tomorrow did offer."

"Is it the hot guy who brought the pizza?"

They think Bentley's hot? "He's forty," I say. "He's not hot."

"He is hot." Nikki nods. "I mean, *I* would never date him, but you totally should."

"It's because he's so hot that I can't," I say. "My husband was already too good-looking for me. I always felt bad around him."

"That's because he was a bas—"

"Oops," I say. "We don't use bad language around here."

Nikki arches one eyebrow like I'm an idiot.

Ricki glances at her sister. "You know that everyone at school says swear words all day long, right?"

"Everyone at school may do that," I say. "But swear words can make people feel unsafe, and with my mother gone, I need this to be a safe place." I realize as I say it that it's actually true. "I won't use bad language with you, and you do the same for me, okay?"

Both of them nod.

Which is way better than a few hours ago.

"And look, I'm going with Bentley as a friend, okay?"

"You're kinda dumb." But Nikki's smiling as she disappears into her room this time.

"She's right." Ricki slows down and stops in the doorway. "But, like, thanks for dinner and stuff." She offers me a half-smile, and it feels like a huge win.

All day the next day, I think about ways I could get out of today's holiday party. It feels like I made a little progress with the girls, and I'm worried it'll be like a turtle hearing a loud noise if I'm not around tonight. They'll duck back in their shells and disappear as soon as I let them.

But Jennifer stops by near the end of the day. She glances at my gold dress, hanging on the edge of my window. "You're ready. Good."

"You're coming?"

She shakes her head. "No, not tonight. Kristy and I are actually going to be at the Goldstone party. You're going with James, and he's going to talk to Quintano about the charges they brought yesterday against Mr. Clark—we want to handle the PR for that case—and you're just supposed to make sure we have a presence for our marketing side. Should be an easy night." She narrows her eyes. "Don't cut out early."

"I won't," I say.

So far, she's pretended like she didn't threaten to fire me, and she's acted like I never said I'd quit. I suppose that's about as good as I can expect. She watches me for a beat or two, and I wonder whether she's going to say something, but she just nods and walks away.

I review the proposal Chump Change has put together for the girls, and I wonder what to do about it. I'm not sure what I *can* do about it. It's not like they covered this in the training—what to do when you're offering money to your foster kid?

I pick up the phone and call Alice.

"Hello?"

"I have a weird question."

"That's not a surprise." She snorts. "If I had a dime for every weird question foster parents called me with. . ."

"You're chipper."

"You haven't called to get rid of them or report that they've attacked you."

"Does that happen a lot?"

"More often than you'd imagine."

"Well, not with these girls. They're hurting," I say.

"They lost their mother and managed to hide it," Alice says. "Did you know that they forged their mother's name on all of the important documents for months now, doing it all under cover of her being under quarantine for being sick?"

"Where's their grandma?"

"She's been dead for eight years. It was a pretty resourceful move."

And it's thoroughly depressing. "Well, look, the reason I was there—"

"They're a client of yours. You said." She grunts. "You're wondering whether they can work for you, now that you're also their guardian."

"Yeah," I say. "I mean, it's not like, a big moral quandary. They've got a super cute Insta account, and they post about their tennis matches and little pranks they play."

"Okay."

"They've been doing things for our clients for almost twenty months now."

"Then why is this even a question?"

"One of our clients wants them to do a commercial," I say. "It's more money, and I think they'll want to do it, and it's not a dicey commercial. They'd play tennis, maybe sing a jingle or something, and promote gum."

"Okay."

"But can I be the one who makes that decision for them, since I'm also the one who's offering them the job?"

"Do you get money from the client for them doing their work?"

"Personally? No. I mean, my company does, and I'm employed by them."

"But you're not paid differently, whether they take the job or not?"

"No."

"And you think they'll want to do it."

"I do."

"Then ask them. But make sure that you put their best interests first."

"You don't think it'll make it less likely that. . ." I feel stupid asking whether it could jeopardize them staying with me. It feels greedy, like I don't want to let them go.

"You want to keep them," she says. "And you want to make sure a judge couldn't use this to deny your request for custody."

"Is that dumb?" I gulp.

"Generally speaking, Barbara, judges and social workers, we're looking for reasons to keep kids in good homes. So unless their dad shows up, or unless their mom isn't really dead, or unless you're secretly some kind of criminal, you're kind of a lock."

I breathe a little easier, knowing I can talk to them about the commercial without worrying that I will need to tell them that they shouldn't do it.

And now it's time to get ready to prance around and smile and act like I'm exactly where I want to be.

When I'm changing in the bathroom, I realize that I forgot my girdle at home. It's fine, but it makes it hard to zip up this dress past my waist, and there's a definite bulge in my middle that I really wish wasn't there.

No matter which way I turn, and no matter how hard I suck in, it's there.

I hate this extra weight.

I know it shouldn't matter. I know Bentley says it's fine, but I'm not blind. I can see that I don't look like I used to, and I promise myself that I'll try and eat a little better and run a little more. I'm tired of looking in the mirror and seeing someone I don't even recognize.

When I pull up at the party, I realize for the first time that it's outside, at a park. It's lovely, actually, and they have space heaters all over. I park my car and navigate the snow-cleared walkway as well as I can in heels. I don't see any super showy sports cars, so I'm pretty sure I beat Bentley here. I contemplate waiting around in the parking lot, but I decide to head for the party. I'm nearly there when Bentley comes jogging up from the other direction.

"Hey." He's breathing heavily.

"Where did you come from?"

"My GPS is fired," he says. "It took me the south route, and then the only parking I could get—never mind." He shakes his head.

I step through to the edge of the party, the heat from the braziers placed every 10 feet hitting me like a palpable wall. I close my eyes and sigh as I undo my coat.

"Wowzer," Bentley says. "That is a *dress*."

I want to wrap my coat back around myself and pretend I'm freezing cold.

"What's wrong?"

There's no way he'd be that nice if he didn't think I needed someone to talk me up. He can clearly see *the bulge*, and he's trying to compensate for it. "Nothing." I force a smile and keep my coat on.

"Are you cold?" He looks around. "Who thought an outdoor event was a great plan?"

"That would be me," Victor Quintano says with a smile.

"Oh," Bentley says. "Well, it's a unique idea."

"I feel like we never get any fresh air in the winter, and the facility here assured me that with the tents and the heaters, we'd be fine." He gestures. "Maybe once you're under the tents it'll be better."

Now I have to take my coat off. I peel it off slowly, trying not to make it obvious that I'm embarrassed. "I'm actually not cold."

Neither of them looks like they believe me, and Quintano's the one who will decide which PR firm they use.

"Really," I say. "It's just that this dress was a little *extra*, and I thought the coat might tone it down a bit."

Bentley takes the coat with a smile. "I recant my criticism about the venue then, and I hope you'll forgive me."

"Of course," Quintano says. "Our firm has dealt with its fair share of misunderstandings lately."

Bentley has no idea what he's talking about, but he rallies well. "I'm sure we all have." He offers me his arm. "And I'll be sure to convince the lady that her extra-dress brings exactly the right amount of holiday cheer."

Quintano raises a glass and nods as he walks off.

"You're pretty good at that," I say.

"After sticking my foot in my mouth," Bentley says, "I can sometimes extricate it reasonably well." His eyes are dancing. "Sorry about that. I'm guessing that guy's important."

I drop to a whisper. "He's the target Jennifer assigned to James for the night."

"Oh, well, then I really did foul up."

"It's fine," I say. "I'm really glad you're here."

"And what's your target for the night?"

"I have to be visible," I say. "That's my task."

"I think we can do visible." Bentley eyes my dress. "With that dress on, you're going to be catching everyone's eye."

I can feel the heat rising in my cheeks. "And now I want my coat back for sure."

"Barbara, tell me you're not still letting that idiot make you feel like you don't look great."

"Stop," I hiss. "Not right now."

"I like you," he says.

I freeze.

"I've liked you for a while." His eyes are intent, and his voice is urgent. "You light up every room you're in. You champion little kids, even when it means your job's put in jeopardy. You're always there for your friends. You're even there for me, and I'm a total nuisance." Bentley's staring right at me, with those big, deep, soul-searching eyes of his. "You're somehow both an anchor and a shooting star, and I have no idea how you manage both, but I'm always in awe of it. I'm not kidding when I say you look amazing. I spend almost all day every day trying to come up with an excuse to touch you." He bites his lip then, and my entire stomach flip-flops.

It's like a scene in a movie.

When Cinderella and the prince stare at each other longingly.

When that girl stands on the pitcher's mound waiting for the guy to kiss her.

When the guy comes walking around the corner with his dog, and he tells the girl he's been the one emailing her all along.

It's *my* moment with Bentley, the one I never thought would happen.

And then James clears his throat, and I realize he was standing behind me.

And all of that was just to make him jealous—of course it was. It worked. There's a muscle popping in his jaw, and he looks like he might actually try to punch Bentley. But the sinking feeling in my heart when I realize Bentley's just doing his job—it's like pulling the plug on Times Square. All the lights in my heart and my mind just blink out.

For the rest of the party, I feel like a wind-up doll, just rocking my way through the motions. I smile. I chat. I talk about how ridiculous the charges against their CFO—who has totally disappeared—must be. I bob my head and smile and talk about how much better they'll do next year.

And all the while, I think about how I thought I was having my moment, but really, I'm just becoming more and more delusional. I think that's my sign. I have got to get out of this deal. The idea was a good one. Shield myself with an old friend so that James can't mess with my heart.

The upshot is that James can't touch me anymore.

I couldn't care less whether he flirts with or kisses or pines after Kristy. They could be celebrating the new year on the table in front of me, naked, and I don't think I would care. But Bentley's breaking my heart in real time, and I just glued it back together. I can't take another crushing blow. I just can't.

Bentley keeps trying to talk to me—he takes my arm, he bumps my hip, and once, he even slides his hand into mine. Those movements mean nothing to him. Just a friend, doing a solid for another friend. But each time, the stupid little tendrils inside my heart try to sprout a little, and I have to crush them with the heel of my boot.

Finally, when it's almost time to go, and he drapes my jacket over my shoulders, I can't do it anymore. "Bentley, I can't." I shake my head. "I can't come to these parties with you anymore."

"What?" He looks panicked for some reason. "Why not?"

"It's too awkward."

"But what I said earlier," he says. "I didn't mean— the thing is—"

"I know." I press my hand against his chest, and even through his suit, I can feel his warmth. I know he's solid, and genuine, and that he wants to help. "I just can't. I'd rather deal with James than—"

"Hey, I hate to interrupt." James looks like he does *not* hate to interrupt. He looks practically irate.

"What?" Bentley asks. "What could you possibly need?"

"We do work together, you know." James crosses his arms.

I normally would agree with Bentley, but right now, I need to get some space from his gorgeous face and big, warm body. "It's fine," I say. "Just go. I'll call you tomorrow, okay?"

Bentley looks like he wants to beat his chest and scream at James, but after balling up his fists, twice, he finally releases his anger, nods quietly, and walks off. He only looks back over his shoulder three times on his way out to Egypt, where he apparently parked.

"Barbara," James says.

"How'd it go with Quintano?" I really hope he doesn't say that I ticked him off.

"Fine," he says. "I think we got the gig, but that's not what I wanted to talk to you about."

"What then?" I start buttoning my coat.

"Barbara." His voice is tense—loaded, even.

"What?" I snap my head up. "What do you want?"

"I made a mistake," he says. "I was so stupid."

"Oh, no." I sigh. "What did you say to him?"

James blinks. "To who?"

"Quintano." Now I'm getting annoyed. I start walking toward my car. He can follow me. "Did you complain about the whole thing being outdoors?"

"No, I don't mean—" He's trotting after me, and it's a little satisfying. Until he grabs my wrist and spins me around.

I nearly lose my footing. "Geez, James. *What?*"

"I'm sorry." He swallows. "I screwed up with Kristy. I know I did."

I blink. "I'm not upset anymore, and I'm sorry to hear things are rocky, but I hardly think I'm the right person to give you relationship advice."

"Barbara, I still love you."

Oh. He's saying *being* with Kristy *is* the mistake. That I did not expect. After the last few days, after my turmoil over Bentley, after trying my hardest to break through with the girls. . .for some reason this strikes me as really, really funny. "You. . .can't possibly be serious." I start to laugh. I mean, I get it under control, but it's comical.

Luckily, my phone bings, providing me a distraction.

It's Bentley. TELL ME YOU GOT TO YOUR CAR. TELL ME THAT CREEP LEFT YOU

ALONE.

My fingers fly over the keys. ACTUALLY, HE JUST PROFESSED HIS LOVE TO ME. I'm sure Bentley will find it as humorous as I do.

"Barbara."

My head snaps up. "James, you're drunk. Go home to Kristy and sleep it off."

"I'm not drunk," he says. "I've been drinking too much lately, because I felt guilty at first, and then because I realized I'd screwed up. Badly."

"Well, that's a real bummer," I say. "Because there's nothing here to save." I gesture between us. "We're already divorced, remember?"

"Get dinner with me," he says. "Tomorrow night."

"I can't," I say.

"Why not? We don't have a holiday party. It's a Sunday. Are you going out with *him*? You just like him because he's minted. You must see that."

"I'm sorry, because he's—what?"

"Minted," James says. "Filthy rich. Loaded."

"I think 'minted' may be a British word, because I've never heard it."

He ignores my hangup with a word that sounds like it would make a great title for an epic holiday romance about a super hot, super rich, debonaire man.

"Barbara, if Bentley was poor, you wouldn't be paying him any attention. And don't forget that he has always had a new girl every weekend. You're just a temporary distraction to him."

"I hardly think that you—"

"Just spare me one night. We were married for close to two years. You can give me one night."

"I can't," I say again. "I have a party tomorrow at Seren and Dave's." The lie just rolls off my tongue.

"I miss them," he says. "I'll come to the party. We

can talk there. I think if you just give me a chance to explain—"

"There you are." Bentley jogs up, draping his coat around my shoulders, like he did with my own coat earlier. "Did you hear the temperature's dropping ten degrees tonight?" He shakes his head. "I can't have my girl freezing to death." He glares at James, who finally mutters something to himself and walks off.

"It's not that cold." I shrug his coat off and try to pass it back.

"Please tell me you aren't considering—"

I shove Bentley just a little, which is a huge overreaction, but I can't have him here, warming me up in every way. The temptation to lean against him is too strong. "Of course not. Don't be stupid. And it's not really dropping ten degrees."

"It is." He points at my car. "Keep the coat."

I almost tell him about Dave and Seren's party that they're apparently throwing tomorrow night, but I decide that I'm better off shutting holiday-madness James down without my bouncer's help. Plus, with the way Bentley's been, he might really punch him. The only thing more pathetic than the way James is acting right now would be a bleeding James who was also whining.

With my soft spot for pathetic things, who knows what I might do then? Something stupid, surely. The last thing I need this year is one more idiotic mistake.

I've made more than enough for the next decade already.

12

BENTLEY

One year, my mom found a tailor who made custom men's dress shirts. My dad wears pajamas every day under his robes, and he hates dressing up, but when Mom had some shirts made for him, he lied and said he loved them.

Every year since, Mom has gotten him another shirt or two.

She has probably put this tailor's kids through college, and as far as I know, Dad has never worn a single shirt. They just hang in his closet, laughing at him. He has to get up before Mom wakes up to make sure she never notices he doesn't have them on, and then he works out on his way home, without fail, every day, so she won't see that he wore athletic clothes into the office. And he has to tell her that his assistant picks up his dry-cleaning.

Or maybe Mom knows he never wears them, but she just keeps buying them anyway. That might be even stranger.

And this feels like that, only worse.

At that holiday party, I finally told Barbara I liked

her. My hands were shaking, and I'd pitted out my shirt underneath my suit coat. Though, that may have had more to do with the massive heat waves from the portable heaters followed by cold wind gusts from being outside.

That Quintano guy's a moron.

But in spite of what I thought was an eloquently phrased, and even rather brave disclosure. . . Barbara thought it was part of this stupid act.

Part of me thinks I should quit pretending. Let her fire me.

But then I have no reason to see her. I'm not confident enough that she likes me to be ready to give up the extra holiday party time.

Which is why, this morning, as soon as I get to the office, I text her. I STILL NEED HELP WITH DATES. I CAN'T LET YOU WIGGLE OUT OF OUR DEAL. LUCKILY, YOU SENT ME THE CALENDAR. I KNOW WHEN THE NEXT PARTY IS.

She doesn't reply.

Which is fine.

I'm not checking my phone every five seconds in an unhealthy way or anything.

"Is there some problem I'm not aware of?" Oliver asks.

I drop my phone like it's on fire. "No."

"Did you get those documents signed?"

"I'll do it now," I say.

But the second he's gone, I pick my phone back up. And it rings. I'm almost smiling. . .when I realize it's only Dave.

"What?" I ask, perhaps with a little too terse a tone.

"Well, hello and Merry Christmas to you too," he

says. "To my oldest friend, let me just tell you how your positive attitude and generosity of spirit has lifted my heart during—"

"Shut up," I say.

"You let me go on way longer than I expected, honestly. In another three words, I'd have run out of stuff to say. I was just calling to invite you to a party tonight."

"How many holiday parties does the world need?" I ask. "Actually, don't answer that. I love holiday parties."

"So. . .you will come? Or are you busy?"

"Wait, who else is coming?"

"I have no idea," Dave says. "And actually, Seren specifically told me not to invite you, but she said I can call and invite Bernie and her idiot friend Corey, who is definitely not getting a call, so I figured I'd pretend that I misheard."

Wait, she specifically told him *not* to invite me? That doesn't sound like Seren. But. . .if her friend told her not to invite me. . . She's as loyal as a lion.

"Is Barbara coming?"

"How should I know?" Dave asks. "Do I sound like the ghost of Christmas future?"

"You sound like you know nothing helpful," I say.

"Why are you such a grouch lately? Are you auditioning for Scrooge in a community theater? Geez."

"I'm not—" I should tell someone, right? No. Yes. "I—"

"You're suffering from cat-got-your-tongue-itis? Did that wife of Emerson convince you to adopt a cat, too? She's a pusher, I swear. I told Seren that if she adopts another cat, I'm going to leave her."

"You won't."

"But she doesn't know that," Dave says.

"Yes, she does."

"You suck, Bentley. Now I know why Seren doesn't want you here." Dave swears under his breath. "If you do come, take a good look at our cats. Two was more than enough, and they got along fine. But when Seren heard there was this Bengal whose elderly owner couldn't manage him—"

"I don't want a cat."

"I said that too, but no one listens to me," Dave says. "So, if you happen to see one who's really, really pretty, I would be willing to part with him. He has green eyes, and he bites your leg if you're too slow to feed him. Not hard, but like, it's annoying."

"You're doing a great job selling me on him."

"Well, you like a dog who's constantly knocking people over and insists on running every day when you hate to run, so who knows what might win you over?"

"I like Barbara."

Complete silence, which I didn't think was possible with Dave on the other end. I've never met a guy who talks as much as he does.

"Did you hear me?"

"I'm sorry, please hold. I'm still processing."

"Process faster."

"Right. Sorry. So you don't want a cat that bites your leg affectionately, but you do like Barbara, Seren's oldest friend. The one who just got divorced and is now fostering two little girls whose mother recently died."

"Yes."

"And you're definitely not supposed to know this, but Barbara's ex is coming over tonight to try and win her back, so now I'm starting to see why Seren told me that you shouldn't come. I'm going to have to rescind my ill-advised invite, and tell you that we're busy tonight."

"I'll be there."

"I'm so screwed," Dave says. "I didn't realize why Seren said you can't come, but now I get it. I really think—"

"Dave."

"What?"

"Shut up." Then I hang up.

Dave was utterly useless, except for telling me that I absolutely have to go to their house tonight. And that I have to bring my A-game.

That loser wants to *win her back*? He threw her away! Is he kidding? My hands ball up even thinking about Mr. Better-than-you Beckham. I'll bend him like. . . Actually, I don't even know if Barbara's loser ex plays soccer. But he *looks* like a soccer wannabe. I can just see him, running around and. . .kicking things.

The rest of the work day feels like an utter slog, and around four o'clock, Oliver kicks me out. "You've been distracted all day. You may as well leave."

"Oh, ho, ho, I didn't know an assistant could kick out his boss."

Oliver's smiling, but he doesn't budge. "We *can* when our bosses clearly aren't able to focus." He tosses his head. "Go."

So I do.

And then, once I'm home, I stare at my closet for a solid twenty minutes trying to figure out what to wear. It's bad enough that I whip out my phone.

I want to call Barbara. She'd know just what I should wear.

But I can hardly ask the person I'm marching into battle to save how to dress. That leaves me very few options. I finally dial Emerson.

"Uncle Bentley?"

"Hey, kid, sorry to bother you."

"Is everything alright?"

"Oh, sure," I say. "Fine. It's just. . ." What am I going to tell him? That I have no idea what to wear? I should've called Dave, but he's worn the same khakis and blue polo shirt to every single event for fifteen years, so he's not exactly a pinnacle of fashion. "Uh, are you going to the party tonight?"

"Are *you*?" Emerson asks.

"I mean, yes," I say. "I am."

"Oh. I thought it was just family."

"Ouch," I say.

"You're family," Emerson says, "but like, just siblings I mean."

"Well, your dad invited me, so." I clear my throat. "I wasn't sure what to wear."

"Wear?" Emerson laughs. "It's literally family. Who cares?"

Who cares. Right. Because in all the time I've known him, I can't think of a single time that I recall even noticing what Emerson was wearing. But now I'm calling him to ask what clothes *I* should put on. To see family.

I've lost my mind.

I need to fix this somehow, or everyone will know I'm unhinged.

"What I mean is, while I'm standing here trying to decide what to wear, I wanted to see if you had ideas for holiday gifts for your family." I cringe a little. I need to get off the phone without making this even weirder.

"Wow, the great Uncle Bentley, the greatest holiday shopper of all time, is asking me for help. This day can't get stranger."

I hang up.

It was the only way out.

When Emerson calls me back, I text and say I have

bad reception. I'm not sure whether he believes me, but I can hope. And finally, defeated, I call Dave.

"Hey, champ. You getting ready?"

"I have no idea what to wear," I say.

"You know, years and years ago, you made fun of me when I couldn't figure out that I liked Seren."

"I did?"

"You did. You threatened me, and you said you'd take her if I didn't man up."

"Well, sounds like I gave you good advice."

Dave harrumphs. "I was getting all prepped to give you a hard time, but now that I'm thinking about it, I guess you did."

"I did."

"So, I'll tell you this instead. I'm wearing a terribly ugly sweater that Seren found at a thrift store. It's covered with slubs of all different colors. I look like a clown."

"A well-loved clown," I say.

"A well-loved clown with the single ugliest reindeer head you have ever seen emblazoned on the front of an already ugly sweater. That means that, no matter what you wear, it can't be worse than what I'm wearing," Dave says. "Come in foot pajamas, and you should still look pretty stylish."

It's not really advice, but it actually helps. "Thanks." I hang up, feeling a little better. I pull out a dark green polo shirt, which looks at least a little festive, and then I grab some dress slacks and shoes. It might be a little too dressy, but after years of doing my most important work in a boardroom surrounded by hostile businesspeople, I feel safer when I'm dressed up.

Of course, by the time I leave, Lucky has both slobbered on and covered my pants with black and white hair, both colors of which show extremely well on grey slacks. Once I finally calm her down, I change to tan slacks. And then I have to change my shoes.

And finally, I'm ready.

At least, I'm as ready as I'm ever going to be. "Okay girl." I crouch down. "Tonight, Dad's going to war." Lucky licks my face. "I need some luck, okay?" She licks me again. "This really bad villain who made Barbara cry, but who she clearly used to like, is going to show up and attack again." She licks me all over, including the inside of my nose. I stand up, rinse off my face, and towel it down. "I'm going to make sure he can't hurt her."

Lucky whines like she understands, and she's on my side.

"And hopefully, I'm going to convince her to date me instead."

Lucky follows me to the door and cries when I leave. It feels like an auspicious send off. Sort of.

On the drive over, I listen to "Eye of the Tiger," because it's always been inspiring to me. I'm going to need to channel all of my best moxie for this moment, because the last time I tried to convince Barbara that I wanted to date her, she blew me off.

Seren clearly went all out at the cottage house for this last-minute party. The inn, as usual, looks *amazing*. It's equal parts Christmas light and house. The holly bush hedges are covered in bright red berries. Large, festive wreaths are hung in every window.

But Seren didn't stop there.

This year, there are smaller but even more festive wreaths hanging in the windows of their cottage house. They have bright plaid bows and little golden stars dangling from them. There's a huge tree on the front lawn that's covered in big, bright, blown-glass-looking ornaments that are probably plastic. They're swaying in the wind.

I check my phone. Is it supposed to snow? It still says no, but the weather feels. . .frosty. I shiver just a bit as I step up to the front porch. The large bears holding presents are standing guard, as usual, with big smiles on their faces. And I can hear the swelling of human chatter mixed with Christmas music coming from just on the other side of the door.

I wonder whether James is already here.

I hope Barbara is.

It would be amazing if I could talk to her *before* he arrives, and then maybe we'd *actually* be dating when that idiot shows up.

It hits me then how upset I really should be. James doesn't know it's fake—me and Barbara. He thinks we're really together, and he's still coming tonight to try and win her back?

I should sock him on the nose.

But would Barbara tell him the truth? Would she get upset with me?

I feel a little like Lucky, pulling on the leash, but worried that my pulling will make my walking buddy mad. It gives me a little more empathy for her. Men really are the eager dogs of the dating world. If we didn't have to think about what the person holding our leash would think, what kinds of crazy things would we do?

Who knows?

I just need to get Barbara to hold my leash.

When I reach for the doorknob, it's already turning. It's Barbara, and I freeze.

"Oh," she says. "I didn't know you—I mean. Come on in." She swallows. She's been wearing fabulous dresses for every holiday party we've attended. Tall heels, sparkles, tight fitted. But tonight, she's wearing dark pants and a red sweater with a reindeer on it, and I kind of love it even more.

"You look great," I say. "Really comfortable. And happy."

She blushes.

Did I say something dumb? Before I can ask, someone else walks up behind me. "Bentley?" It's James. I've come to hate his stupid British accent more than I hate people asking me to take a five-minute research survey.

I turn around slowly. "What are *you* doing here?"

He holds up a large metal bowl. "Seren brought some kind of trail mix stuff to our housewarming party, and then she left it. Remember?"

"Muddy buddies," I say. "Hers are famous, but Seren has never made trail mix in her life."

"Whatever," James says. "When I heard there was a party, I figured I could bring the bowl back."

I yank the bowl out of his hands. "Thanks. Got it. You can go."

James frowns. "You have gotten so rude that I can't even write it off as general American bad manners."

"No, it's more like 'irritated boyfriend dealing with the unwanted ex,'" I say. "Are Brits super nice to their girlfriend's exes over there?" I feign a bad British accent. "Do you invite them in for tea?"

"Bentley," Barbara says, the same way I say "Lucky" when I'm warning her.

She's tugging on my leash.

Maybe that's a good sign? "Fine," I say. "Come on in." I swing the door wide and step through, slinging an arm around Barbara's shoulders.

"Gee, thanks," James says as he walks through the door.

"What's your husband doing here?" Nikki asks.

"I thought you divorced him," Ricki says.

"I did," Barbara says. "But we still work together."

"But this isn't work," Nikki says. "So why are you here?" She frowns.

James stops just past the doorway, staring blankly at the two girls.

"Why are the double twins here?" he asks, his head turning slowly toward Barbara.

"Are you going to be our new daddy?" Ricki steps closer, her eyes wide. She brings her hands into a prayer position. "I always wanted a British daddy."

"And I've always wanted a pony." Nikki's beaming too. "Will you buy me one for Christmas?"

"Did someone say pony?" Emerson's new wife, Elizabeth, turns around. "Because a friend of mine has this gorgeous black pony for sale at the barn, and if you want a pony for a kid, Fuego is *the* one you want."

James' eyes widen. "What on earth—"

"Barbara's fostering Nikki and Ricki right now," I say. "You didn't hear?"

Barbara shakes my arm off and walks toward the girls. "That's enough messing around, you two."

"What?" Nikki says. "You *don't* want to be our daddy?" Her grin's pure evil, and I love her for it.

"Stop," Barbara hisses.

"I thought that would work better than punching him," Ricki says. She's not smiling. She looks dead serious.

"Can we talk for a minute?" James points at the office.

"What do you want to talk about?" Ricki asks.

I'm ready to adopt her.

"Adult stuff," James says.

"If you want her to date you again. . ." Ricki shakes her head. "Just remember. She's not that stupid."

I can't help laughing.

Barbara glares, but that just makes me laugh harder.

"Look, all I'm saying," Nikki says, "is if I had to pick between that guy." She points at me. "And you?" She shrugs. "Hands down, pick the rich guy who's nice."

I high five her.

"It's fake," Barbara says. "Bentley and I made a deal that he'd escort me to holiday parties to pay me back for helping him figure out online dating."

Now every single person in the room is staring.

"You—it was—a deal?" James glares at me, like *I'm* the villain.

And I want to sink into the carpet.

After James goes into the study with Barbara on his heels, I look around the room for something to destroy. Luckily, Seren intercepts my rage-filled fuming by handing us all bowls of popcorn and cranberries. "Let's make some garland, shall we?"

I've stabbed my finger three times with the blunt-tipped needle when Nikki takes it away from me. "There are some times when men shouldn't be armed. I think this is one of them."

"Yeah," Ricki says. "You look a little stabby to be holding that."

"I can't believe she's talking to that guy," I mutter, realizing that I should not be talking to these little girls about this. "But let's talk about Christmas, huh? Are you guys ready?"

"Do you like her?" Nikki asks. "Because it kind of looks like you do, and you did help her trick us that night."

"Then you stuck around for a long time after,"

Ricki says. "And you dug through trash and ignored a lot of rats."

"I like you way better than that guy." Nikki flings her thumb backward at the door. "Even if he does sound cooler than you."

"Why does everyone love a British accent so much?" I ask. "Their drinks are always room temperature, and they spell everything wrong."

"James Bond's British," Jake says as he walks in from the back room. "I think that's why everyone likes the accent so much."

Bea rolls her eyes.

"Oh good. Everyone's in here now." I am so glad this can be a family discussion.

"I'm not sure how Uncle Bentley feels is any of our business," Seren says. "I think it's between Bentley and Barbara."

"We live with her, though," Nikki says. "I think we deserve to know."

"And I really want to know, too." Elizabeth leans closer to the girls. "Keep asking questions. Barbara's really tough, but Bentley's a softie. I think we can crack him."

"Elizabeth," Emerson says. "Come on."

"I want to know too," Bea says. "I've wondered for years why two amazing people like them didn't date." Her eyes are sparkling. "This is just the most exciting night."

"For the love—" Dave says. "Honey, turn the holiday music up higher."

"So do you like her?" Ricki asks. "Or not?"

And now everyone's looking at me—even Killian, who had been hiding in the corner with his headphones on. I realize that he may have been pretending not to listen while he was really paying attention the whole time. Teenagers are the worst.

"I do like her," I finally say. "It took me long enough to realize it, but—"

"Why *did* it take you so long?" Jake asks. "Now that I have lots of money, will I get stupid, too?"

That kid needs to be punched a few times. Maybe he'll stop running his mouth so much. "Now I've actually told her how I feel," I say, "she persists in thinking I'm just playing my part."

"How did you tell her, though?" Jake asks.

"Yeah," Killian says. "Was it, like, 'hey, let's hang out?' Because my friend Dana says that a lot of guys do that, and it's annoying. You should just tell her you want to date her and that you're serious about it."

I look at the ceiling, hoping for a little patience. "I was very clear," I say. "But she thanked me, because that idiot—" I throw my thumb over my shoulder. "Walked up right behind me. I think she thought I was saying stuff so that he'd overhear."

"James is still screwing things up now?" Seren shakes her head. "He really is the worst."

"Are we sure it's really a good time to tell her how you feel?" Dave asks. "Maybe it's good that she didn't understand you."

"Yeah, maybe you should wait a bit," Seren says. "It's been a really bad year."

"Isn't that when you need good news the most?" Bea asks.

"It's not like he's showing up on her door with a big check," Dave says.

"A big check?" Killian asks. "Why would he bring a big check?"

"Because he's rich," Ricki says. "Everyone likes a rich guy. That's a good idea."

"No." Dave shakes his head. "I'm talking about the Publisher's Clearinghouse thing. That big check he can barely carry that Ed McMahon brings?"

Everyone in the room, other than me and Seren, just stares at him blankly.

"Never mind all of that," I say. "Look, I don't know whether to press it, or just leave it alone for now."

"Tell her again," Ricki says. "Sometimes girls need to be told things a lot."

"Don't do it," Jake says. "She'll just reject you if she's not ready, and then things will be super weird. Tonight has already been weird enough."

"But," Bea says, "if she doesn't know he's serious—"

Seren and Dave, Elizabeth and Emerson, and even Killian all have opinions, and they're all sharing them, and I have no idea what anyone's saying when the door from the office opens abruptly.

James has his hands shoved into his pockets, and he's looking at the floor when he marches through. . .and walks right out the front door. That's good news, at least.

"So you told him to take a hike?" Dave asks, the second the door closes.

Bless him.

"I told him that he and I were a bad idea from the start," Barbara says. "And that it's best if we don't try to reopen that Pandora's box."

"You should've let Bentley hit him," Ricki says. "That would've been way cooler."

Jake laughs and ruffles the hair on Ricki's white-blond head. "You're alright, kid."

Ricki flushes bright red and swallows.

"Knowing James, he'd have sued Bentley," Barbara mutters.

It would have been worth it.

"Yeah, but he's rich," Nikki says. "He could have paid him."

"And then James would have Bentley's money," Dave says. "Better that Barbara just sent him packing."

"Aaand that's way more time talking about my ex than I like," Barbara says. "What were you guys doing while I was in there? Making garland?" She looks at my string, which has three pieces of popcorn, one of them a little red from my blood, and one smooshed cranberry. Then she turns slowly to look at Seren's, which has double that. No one else has even started a strand. "No one's. . .done one yet?"

Elizabeth laughs, but it sounds forced. "Well, Bentley stabbed his finger."

"Where's Ardath when you need her?" Barbara asks. "And speaking of things that I don't understand, why's the holiday music so loud?"

Seren shifts over so she can turn it down. "Ardath's coming, but she had a late shift, so—"

As if she was summoned, Ardath breezes through the front door. "Was that James I just saw leaving?" Her nose is scrunched. "Please tell me he's not back."

"Did no one like him?" Barbara asks. "Why didn't you guys tell me this stuff before I married him?"

"We like Bentley," Emerson says.

And everyone in the room now looks really, really uncomfortable. Which is exactly how I feel. It's not like everyone thinks it's a good idea. They're all split. And what happens if I swing for the fences. . .and Barbara turns me down? Then am *I* the one who gets cut out, like stupid James?

It's not a comforting thought.

By the time we've all made a string of garland, Seren's pumpkin cookies have come out of the oven, and Ardath has made her pretzel pecan crunchy candy things, and the music's blasting "I'll be Home for Christmas," and it feels like we've almost recovered from the horribly awkward conversation I caused.

"So what time are we getting together on Christmas Eve?" I ask.

Dave bites his lip.

Seren half-cringes.

They lock eyes.

Emerson and Elizabeth are also sharing some kind of weird look.

"We're all going on a cruise this year," Bea finally says.

"It's my fault," Elizabeth says. "I mentioned that I'd always wanted to do something like that for Christmas, and then Emerson's grandmother booked us all on the Celebrity cruise out of Stockholm without even really confirming we could all go, but she did pay for it, and it does sound really cool."

"Out of. . ." I'm confused. "Wait, so you'll *all* be gone?"

"She booked Mom and Dad and all the siblings," Emerson says. "And it happened so fast."

"You didn't do anything wrong," Barbara says. "I think it's great you're all going."

But neither she nor I have had a Christmas Eve that *wasn't* at Dave and Seren's in. . .fourteen or fifteen years, probably. Not since they got Emerson. "Right," I say. "I mean, it's totally fine."

"You guys said you didn't want to celebrate Christmas this year anyway," Barbara's saying to Ricki and Nikki.

At the exact same time as I say, "We should do Christmas at my house instead, then."

But then I freeze. Because the girls said they don't

want to celebrate. And now I'm sticking my foot right in it. "Uh, never mind."

"Actually, I do want to go to Bentley's," Ricki says. "I think that sounds fun. Can we have hot chocolate and make a snowman?"

"I can't promise the snowman," I say. "That's kind of up to Mother Nature, but I can offer lots of kinds of hot chocolate."

"Our mom always made it from real chocolate, in a pot," Nikki says, her voice super quiet.

"I can show Bentley how to do that," Seren says.

"That would be—are you sure?" Barbara asks.

In that moment, I'm entirely sure. And I've also made up my mind. I'm going to tell Barbara how I feel on Christmas Eve. Between the holiday spirit and the adorable little girls, and my dog showing her what a good guy I am, how could it go wrong?

13

BARBARA

My mom loved Christmas. She usually had the tree up before Halloween, and she didn't even bother putting orange lights on it or anything. She bought more ornaments for that poor tree every year, until it was almost bowed down to the ground with them.

Mom made us go caroling every year, even though it's freezing in New York and it was clear that people didn't want to stand there with their door open for ten minutes. She made a dozen different kinds of holiday cookies. She strung lights on her porch, on her bushes, and on the trunks of her trees. Basically, she put them anywhere she could without Dad risking falling off a ladder and breaking his neck.

She always picked a family to surprise with little gifts every day for the twelve days leading up to Christmas Day. When I was a kid, I loved racing to the front door to leave them something and then rushing back to the car, hoping not to be caught.

Mom brought holiday cheer with her everywhere she went.

You'd think I'd be aching to do the same, especially now that she's gone. I kind of am, actually, but the girls haven't really revisited the issue since slamming the door in my face, so the lights are still in a pile by the tree, and it's still in a bucket. No other decorations have even been hauled up from my apartment-assigned storage area.

Nikki looks like she may nod off in the car, and I'd rather not have them fall asleep just before we get back home.

"I'm surprised you wanted to visit Bentley for Christmas," I say on the way home.

Nikki's eyes shoot open. "Why?"

"Well, my mom loved Christmas," I say. "After she died." I shrug. "I'm not sure. My love for the decorations and stuff, it all just made me think of her. And thinking of her hurts."

"Our mom loved Christmas too," Ricki says. "But that's not why we wanted to skip it this year."

"You want*ed* to skip it?" I ask. "As in, now you don't?"

"I'm excited to go to Bentley's," Ricki says. "I like him. Don't you?"

"But why did you want to skip it before?" I refocus on a question for which I'm comfortable searching for the answer. "You said you want*ed*, implying that now you don't."

"Well." Nikki shrugs. "Our dad and mom were together until a few years ago."

A few years ago?

"Yeah," Ricki says. "Back when he was still around sometimes, Dad actually bought us all this stuff one year. He was super duper excited. We helped him wrap some stuff for Mom, too."

"Okay."

"But then," Nikki says, "on Christmas morning, he was just *gone*."

"Gone?" I can't help my frown. I hope they can't really see it in the rearview mirror, which is the only way they can see me right now.

"He smiled his way through us opening the presents and then he said he had to go to the bathroom. We waited like half an hour, and then we went to check on him," Ricki says. "We found a note on the bathroom counter. He'd gone out the window, I guess. It said, 'I wanted to give you the best Christmas ever, but I can't.'" She shakes her head. "And then he was just gone."

"Everything is like that," Nikki says. "Sometimes something really good will happen, but when it does." She sighs.

"Something really, really bad always happens right after," Ricki says.

I wonder whether they've realized how often they finish each other's sentences.

"I think those were just coincidences," I say. "It's not really how life works. As you get older, plenty of good things will happen, without any bad things happening right after."

Nikki and Ricki look at each other, and I can tell they don't believe me.

"When else did bad stuff follow good?"

"Oh, lots of times. But recently, Mom had lost a few jobs," Nikki said. "But then she got a great one. She was in charge of development for wreaths for this home decor company, and she got to design them all day. It was her favorite thing to do."

"And a week after she got the job, we found out she was sick," Ricki says. "One week."

"Yes, but—"

"We want to go see Bentley," Nikki says. "But can you maybe tell him not to get us any presents?"

It breaks my heart, seeing how nervous they are for anything wonderful to happen in their lives.

"Speaking of good things, I haven't told you two this yet, but there's a gum company that wants to do a remake of an old commercial, and they'd like to use you to do it. Retro stuff is back, and they think it'll be a big hit."

Nikki shakes her head. "Can we say no?"

I'm just floored. "Don't be silly. Listen, this is great news, and it pays well."

"Do you need the money?" Ricki looks nervous.

"No," I say. "I'd put all the money into an account for you two, and you can use it when you go to college."

"If you don't need the money, can we say no?" Nikki looks absolutely adamant.

Luckily, we're just pulling into the parking lot. I pick a spot and kill the car. Then I turn all the way around to face them. "Girls."

They both look pretty scared.

"I know that it's hard sometimes, and that bad things can leave us scared." I sigh. "But I've been giving this a lot of thought. I know I'm just your emergency home right now, but I'd like to be your permanent home. I've been taking extra classes during my lunch break, and I have my basic certifications done. I'd like to be your permanent foster mom, if you'll have me. And I promise that I'll make sure nothing terrible happens after good things do, from now on, okay?"

Ricki starts to cry.

Nikki looks about an inch away from it.

"You don't have to stay with me if you don't want to, though," I say. "And they're still looking for your dad."

Ricki shakes her head. "We want to stay with you. We hate our dad."

"Well, you shouldn't hate him," I say. "We don't know what he was dealing with—"

"He's a jerk," Nikki says. "Like, we didn't even like him when he was coming around sometimes."

"Well, people can change, but I won't change my mind about this. I'd really love to keep you as long as you want to be with me."

Nikki lunges forward, her arms thrown out to hug me, but her seatbelt throttles her. She swears under her breath, and then her head pops up. "Sorry. I'm trying not to say them."

I laugh. "Life's a process. It's fine."

Ricki has unbuckled, and she hugs me, her arms snaking around the chair to squeeze me. "I want to stay with you."

After Ricki releases me, I look at Nikki. "And how about you?

She's unbuckled too, and she zooms forward and hugs me as well. "Yes."

I can't help my smile. "But I'm not promising not to get you presents, and I think you should accept the commercial. Then, by New Years, maybe you'll believe that plenty of good things can happen without any bad, okay?"

Both girls nod, but they both look nervous. After they've brushed their teeth and they're in pajamas, I go into their room to tuck them in.

"You won't change your mind, will you?" Nikki asks. "Like, if you got a boyfriend, and if he didn't like us, then would you send us away?"

My half-smile's wry. "I doubt I'll be finding a boyfriend any time soon, but if he was so dumb that he didn't like you, you better believe he'd be kicked to the curb right quick."

Ricki looks like she might cry again.

"I know I haven't known you very long," I say. "But I love you girls already." And now I'm crying, too. "I'm happy you want to stay with me."

"What if our dad shows up?" Ricki asks. "Can you kick him to the curb too?"

They're asking so many complicated questions. "I can't speak to that," I say. "It wouldn't be up to me. But I think the Court is smart enough to know how to handle that kind of thing, alright?"

Ricki nods slowly. "Okay. But for Christmas, you're letting us go over to celebrate with Bentley?"

I don't tell them that I have no one else to celebrate with. No parents. My only friends on a cruise. My ex-husband officially told off again. "Yes, we can. I think you'll like his dog."

"He has a dog?" Nikki perks up. "What kind?"

"It's black and white and it licks a lot." I shrug.

"Maybe it's a terrier," Ricki says.

"Or a corgi. They come in black and white," Nikki says.

"It's bigger and fluffier than those," I say. "But I'm sure he remembers—"

"Is it a border collie?" Ricki asks. "They have a lot of energy and a lot of them are great with frisbees." Her eyes are so bright, they could practically light up the room.

"Do you girls love dogs?"

"We've always wanted one," Nikki says, "but Mom was allergic."

"Ah, well, I'll text him and ask, alright?"

Both of them nod.

"Now, go to sleep. Maybe after school next week, we can go shopping for something for Bentley."

"Yeah, that's a good idea," Nikki says.

"It's actually a bit of a chore," I say. "Bentley's hard to shop for. You two can try to help me pick something for the guy who has everything."

They look at each other and smile, for some reason. I have no idea why.

"What?"

They both start giggling.

"Okay, off to bed."

It takes them almost half an hour to get quiet, but finally they do, and I breathe a sigh of relief. I call Seren to tell her how our conversation went, and she's as excited as I am.

"You know, Emerson turned us down when we wanted to adopt him."

"I was there," I say. "Remember?"

"Oh, right." Seren laughs. "Dave had you videotape it. His epic fail."

"Not so much a fail," I say. "You said yes."

"I knew nothing about kids like Emerson then," Seren says. "You know so much more than I did."

"But you and Dave have done such an amazing job," I say. "And I'm the world's biggest screw up."

"The great thing about these kids," Seren says, "is that they've already dealt with so much crap, that all a lot of them need is a whole bucket of love. They'll forgive any other mistakes you make."

That makes me cry all over again.

"I wonder if it's a mistake to go to Bentley's," I say, when I finally get myself together. "It's a lot for a single guy to handle."

"They'll like the dog," Seren says. "Plus, who else

does Bentley have to buy presents for? Let him spend some of his money on those cute girls."

"Speaking of," I say. Then I tell her about their aversion to gifts.

"So you're going to bury them under things and let them see that they're wrong, right?" Seren asks.

"Something like that," I say. "Although, my bank account is much thinner than I am. I told Santa I wanted a big bank account and a small tush last year, and I think he mixed them up."

Seren laughs.

"But for real, anything they get will be great, I think. Based on what they had in their apartment, they haven't had many great Christmases. I plan to take them shopping for new clothes, too. Some of theirs are pretty tatty."

"They may have memories connected to them, though," Seren says. "So don't push them to get rid of anything yet."

"Great," I say. "I've adopted two hoarders."

"You have no idea how many memories can be attached to something, even something stupid," Seren says.

As I'm looking at an old, tired, dusty wreath my mom gave me, I realize she's wrong. "No, I do."

"Crap, Barb, I forgot about your parents for a second. I'm sorry."

"It's fine," I say. "Really. I know what you meant."

"The only thing that's going to heal those girls is the same thing that's fixing you right now."

"What?" I'd really like to know what that is.

"Time," Seren says softly. And that's when I remember just how much I love her. She always understands, but she also offers real insight when I need it.

"Thanks," I say. "I just wish it could go a little faster. And slow down."

"Yeah, time's strange like that," Seren says. "No matter what we want, it just keeps marching along at the same pace."

"If you have gift ideas for eleven-year-old girls, can you send them over?" I ask. "I'm coming up a little blank."

"You're taking them shopping for something for Bentley?" Seren asks.

"Yes."

"Watch what they touch and look at and comment on."

"Brilliant." She's so smart.

"But I'll also ask Killian what the girls just a little younger than his friends love, and I'll let you know what he says."

"Thanks."

"I've been a mom for a while now," Seren says. "I'm glad you're finally joining the ranks. Best gig in the world."

"I loved being an aunt, but this is different. Scarier, but also better, in a lot of ways." My heart expands in that moment, and I realize that it's true. Most people would want to dive into a new relationship after ending the last, but I think what I needed was to take care of someone else. "I think it's helping me realize that I'm not just a useless, fat lump."

"You're not useless," Seren says automatically.

"As my best friend, you have to say that," I say.

"But it's still the truth," she says. "And furthermore, I'm in possession of some knowledge that you might want. It could change your whole perspective."

I doubt that, but now I have to know. "Knowledge?"

"What would obtaining top secret information be worth to you?" Seren asks.

"What?" I have no idea what to offer. "You're always the one giving me things already. You bake, you give advice, and you usually host. I bring nothing to the table."

"For heaven's sake," Seren says. "Are we spiraling again?"

But I realize that even if it's a little *Eeyore,* what I said was totally right. I've never done anything for Seren. I'm not even sure why she's my friend.

"Barb, you tidy my house every time you come. You babysit my kids and have for years, for free, whenever I needed a hand. You've watched them for a whole week on four separate occasions when Dave's parents couldn't so Dave and I could get away. You bring me snacks from my favorite places constantly. You help us with marketing for the inn. You've given me feedback on ads, on fliers, on events, on room decor, and on relationship complications. You have been there for me in every single way for almost thirty years."

Now she's making me bawl.

"I hate that little jerk for making you feel like that," Seren says. "I'm glad you kicked him to the curb."

"He only came over because he was jealous," I say. "He threw his toy away, but he thinks some big, rich, talented guy likes me." I laugh. "Which is the real joke, because I blurted out that Bentley's just doing me a favor, so now he knows how pathetic I really am."

"But he's not," Seren says. "That's the big secret. Bentley Harrison is in love with you, Barbara, and everyone knows it's true *except* for you. James can tell, too. That's why he's been so insane lately—that's the real reason he showed up. He could sense that it wasn't fake. At least, not on Bentley's end."

"No way," I say. "You're delusional."

"Nope," she says. "You're the one who's not accepting reality."

"Look, you guys have wished he would like me for years, but that doesn't mean—"

"He announced it to the entire room, including your two little girls. They *clearly* agreed to visit him for Christmas because they want you to find out, too. That means they like him, by the way, and that's a really good sign. A lot of girls in their situation would be jealous of anyone who might take your attention from them. They're healthy enough to realize that a happy Barbara is a good thing for them."

I'm speechless for a moment, but when I'm able to form words again, I splutter. "Seren, that's insane. I'm sure he was just—"

"No. Stop it right now. I already gave you one pep talk today, so listen carefully when I say this. You spent half an hour earlier telling me how silly those poor, broken little girls are being about thinking that bad stuff always follows good stuff. You told me they need to get their world view corrected, and you're going to do it. But you're dumber than they are. You think Bentley Harrison can't like you because he's rich, he's handsome, he's smart, and he's funny. You think someone like that could never like *you*. Well, you're wrong. As an outsider, I can tell you that you're generous, you're caring, you're capable, and you're smart."

"I'm not beautiful, though," I say. "I notice you left that out."

"You're not beautiful," Seren says. "You're *stunning*. You have the kind of obvious beauty that I always envied. You're like a Barbie doll. You're like a print ad model."

"You're being absolutely idiotic right now," I say. "Have you looked in a mirror?"

"I know." Seren sniffs. "I've always hated my stupid face—thanks a lot, grandma—and you were the only girl I knew who was friends with me anyway. You were so stunning that you stood out, even by my side. Because you're *spectacular,* Barbara Champion. You used to know that, and it's time for you to get your confidence in yourself back. Because when you find it again, there's a guy who's actually worthy of you. And he's waiting. I'm just not sure how long he'll wait for." Seren pauses. "Don't miss it because you don't believe in yourself anymore. That would be a really tragic way for James to win."

❧ 14 ❧

BENTLEY

High bars are the worst.

I like to be the best at whatever I do. That means I'm always setting high bars, but then in order to be great, I have to clear those bars again later. That bumps it up higher, and higher, and higher.

The bar for me on gift giving has gotten stupid high, and now it's giving me anxiety.

To make matters worse, society has these expectations you have to think about. If you spend too much money, you've crossed a line. That means I need to find things people want, even if they don't know they want them. Or I have to locate things they can't find. But, it still needs to be something that will matter to them and show that I care. Add in that, for the first time in my life, I really, *really* like someone, and I'm basically a basketcase at the thought of finding her the perfect gift.

The first Christmas I spent with Seren and Dave, after they got married, I found out that Barbara liked books. Classic literature's her favorite, though she reads enough that sometimes she even reads total junk, like horse shifter romance or even stranger, dragon shifter romance. I cannot, for the life of me, understand why a woman would want to date someone who could turn into an *animal* or *creature*, but that's not the craziest thing I don't understand about women, so. . .

It took me three weeks to find a first edition of *Jane Eyre*. It was worth it, though, because Barbara was delighted. Seren glared at me quite a lot for upstaging her—at least, until she opened her Miyabi knife set. I was actually a little worried that I'd outshone her and then armed her with very sharp cutlery, but her glee at getting the knives overpowered her irritation.

She went and carved up some figs for tarts instead of my face, so we were all happy. I know Barbara well enough to have some decent ideas, but one thing about which I know almost nothing: preteen girls. And I definitely don't want to show up Barbara, so in my zeal to see Barbara over the holidays, I've found myself in a bit of a sticky situation.

I spend three days shopping, but I'm still not sure I've struck the right tone. Barbara canceled on me for the last two holiday parties on her calendar, and I'm trying not to read too much into that, but I may have lost some ground in the past week. She keeps blowing me off, and I want to give her space to be a mother, but I don't want to back off so much that she forgets about me.

I need to come in clutch with the perfect gifts. I'm walking past store after store, agonizing a bit, when Oliver has had enough, apparently. We're just outside of Tiffany's when he stops, like a donkey pulling against its lead, jutting out his jaw.

"I'm going back to the *office*," he says. "You know, that place where we used to actually do meaningful work? Before we spent all our time pining and shop-ping and pining more?"

"I have employees," I say. "Even when I'm not there, stuff's still getting done. You used to get mad at me for micromanaging."

"This is going nowhere, though." He sighs. "You've already spent a tremendous amount of money. Are you thinking there will be something in one of these places that just reaches out and grabs you. *Buy me for Barbara?*" He shakes his head in disgust. "Because that's not going to happen."

But as he's ranting, I look over his shoulder, and I see a sign inside the store behind him. It's huge. It's lovely. And it says, "For the Love of your Lifetime."

My lifetime. Not my life. My *entire lifetime.*

That's it.

It's like the sign is reminding me of something that I knew I wanted, but I wasn't sure exactly how to get— I should buy Barbara an *engagement* ring. I don't just want to give her something great that convinces her to date me. I've known her for fifteen years, for heaven's sake.

I want to marry her.

If pop culture has taught me anything, it's that if I like it, which I do, then I better put a whopping huge ring on it. Otherwise some idiot like James or that Davis guy will grab her before I can.

And I do like her. I *love* her.

"You can go back," I say.

"No." Oliver follows the line of my vision and then grabs my shoulder. "You're not even dating, man. You *cannot* propose to her. You said it yourself—she's spooky. You *will* scare her off."

"I think I know her better than you do." I yank

myself free and walk toward Tiffany's. "You've only met her twice."

"A dozen times at least," Oliver says, "but believe me. If you think this is the way to go, then I do know her better. She just got divorced."

The entire store's drowning in holiday lights, holly berries, snowmen, and fake-snow topped stuff. "No." I'm absolutely positive. "This is *it*. I'm going to buy the very nicest ring in this store, and she's going to say yes, and by New Years, I'll be engaged." I'm beaming even wider than the stupid clerk who's probably getting a BMW down-payment as his commission as I buy a beautiful, cushion-cut solitaire, with a delicately braided band that looks like an actual work of art. "The stone's flawless, right?"

The cashier nods.

"Because this girl is flawless. The stone has to match."

And when I walk out, ignoring Oliver's stupid histrionics the entire way, I'm finally ready for Christmas Eve. The caterers and the decorator leave about an hour before the girls are set to arrive—Lucky has been beside herself, so it's good she'll have a bit to recover. I take her for a walk outside—no snow. No snowmen for the girls, but that's out of my control.

"Alright, girl." Once we get back inside, I sit down and let Lucky practically lick my face off. "Get all that manic energy out, because when they get here, I can't have you mauling our guests. Tonight has to go *perfectly*, or—"

The doorbell rings. Twelve minutes early—could that be them already?

It is.

I can't help beaming just a little as I swing the door wide open.

"You're in a coat," Barbara says. "Were you going out?"

"Just getting in," I say. "I took Lucky for a walk."

"Oh." She nods. "Great."

"She *is* a border collie," Ricki says. "Told you."

"Actually, I said I wasn't sure," Barbara says. "And then I kept forgetting to ask Bentley what kind of dog she is."

"Border collie's right," I say. "And be prepared." She's already wagging her tail nub like she's preparing to launch. "She likes to jump up, and she loves to lick people right on the face."

"Bring it," Ricki says. "I like all of that."

"Dog energy is good energy," Nikki says.

Barbara holds out her hands, and I realize she brought something.

"What's this?" I ask as I take it from her. With the saran wrap on top, it's hard to really see what's on the tray.

"It's a cheeseball," she says. "Mom always made one, and since she always did it, I'm not quite as good as her, and I know you said I didn't need to bring—" She's taking her coat off, and she freezes. Her eyes are locked on the dining room table and the server buffet where all the appetizers and desserts are laid out.

"Oh, that?" I shrug. "That's just stuff from the caterers. I don't really cook, so Seren made me a recommendation, but I'm super excited for this cheeseball." I start unwrapping it, and I set it down next to the spinach and artichoke dip and stuffed mushrooms. "Plus, these crackers are my favorite." I sniff. "They're the sun-roasted tomato Wheat Thins, right?"

Barbara nods absently, still looking at the cheeseball with a wistful expression.

"What's wrong?"

"It looks funny next to all that stuff," Nikki says. "It's all wonky and misshapen, and she didn't cut the pecans right."

Now that she points it out, I notice what she means. The crackers are all bunched up on one side, whereas the crackers next to the artichoke dip are artfully splayed. The cheeseball is a little lumpy looking, and it's more noticeable next to the perfection of the catered, professionally prepared food.

"Who cares about that?" I ask. "I'm a guy. All I care about is how it tastes."

But Barbara has already snatched the saran wrap out of my hand and she's trying to wrap the cheeseball back up. "Let's just stick it in the fridge. I can take it home when we go and eat it later."

I take it from her. "No. You brought that for me, and I want my cheeseball. Leave it alone. No takebacks."

"What, are you twelve?" She glares at me for a moment, but then she turns to face the girls. "There's a coat closet right here."

"That's pretty fancy," Nikki says. "At home we just pile them on the—"

"And here are the gifts." Ricki thrusts a bag at me.

"Hey," I say. "I thought we agreed that I'd give you guys stuff, but you didn't have to bring anything."

"Yeah, that was a nice idea," Barbara says. "But there was never a chance we were going to let you provide dinner, the venue, and gifts and not give you something."

"Well, thank you." I carefully take four gifts out of the bag and place them next to the rest of mine under the tree.

"Wow," Ricki says. "Your gifts all look *amazing*."

Her eyes are round, and I try to see it like she must. My tree this year is all silver and gold, perfectly decorated, and the gifts underneath it are wrapped in matching, coordinated paper. Gold. Patterned gold. Silver. Patterned silver. And two prints that have both.

"Yeah, the thing is, my office manager found someone who does decor and stuff, and she just. . ." I shrug. "Does it all."

"That's amazing." Nikki's digging her toe into the carpet. "I wrapped mine, so it's really ugly. Sorry."

I glance at the gifts I just set down, and I notice that they're all in different paper. One is red, with the ends bunched up. One is green, and whoever wrapped that used *way* too much tape. The other two are silver and gold, and green and red. They were clearly wrapped by Barbara, but even with their adorable bows, they don't look professional.

"Your presents look way better than all of mine," I say. "Because they look personal. They were wrapped by *you*."

But no one speaks as we walk into the dining room. "I'm assuming you guys are hungry," I say. "Because I'm starving."

"Sure," Nikki says. "I am, too."

Thankfully, dinner goes a lot better than their arrival. I make a point of moving the cheeseball to the table, where it's the only appetizer, and we all carve off a big chunk of it. The girls love the turkey, and they get seconds, and Barbara eats lots of ham.

"That's one of the only good things about Seren being out of town," Barbara says. "I don't feel guilty about eating meat."

"Do you usually?" I ask.

"Always," Barbara says. "Since I was a kid." She

shakes her head. "What? You don't?" She laughs. "On our first date, you said you might give up meat."

"I was just trying to get to Dave," he says. "I knew he liked her, even then."

"How?" Barbara looks genuinely curious. "I've always wondered that."

"How many times do you think Dave set me up?" I arch an eyebrow. "In all the years I've known him?"

She shrugs.

"Never," Ricki blurts, a green bean shooting out of her mouth and landing in the mashed potatoes in front of us. She freezes, her eyes glued to the big blob of green on the perfect mountain of white.

She looks absolutely horrified, so of course I can't help laughing.

"You just spit in the potatoes," Nikki says. "Say sorry!"

I shake my head. "Please don't," I say. "Earlier, I dropped a whole blob of gravy on the tablecloth. You guys are just doing me a favor." I mock-whisper the next part. "I always feel like the proverbial bull in the china shop at fancy meals."

"You do?" Ricki asks.

I nod slowly. "And you were totally right. Dave never once asked me to go on a double date, not before that one, and never again since. I knew the second he did that, that something weird was going on. Once I saw her, and I saw the way he looked at her?" I shrug. "I knew he was a goner."

"That's pretty cute," Barbara says. "I just wish I'd known how Seren felt. I think I must've called and texted Dave twenty times. It was pretty embarrassing."

"Oh, I don't think so," I say. "If he hadn't met Seren, you'd have been the hottest, smartest person he'd ever had the luck to meet."

"I've never been able to measure up to my best friend, though," Barbara says. "I've always been an idiot —for being such good friends with someone so much better than me."

"You're the kind of person who likes to build people around you up, and that's something to be proud of. You're also not afraid to surround yourself with excellence, and that's also rare." I shake my head. "But actually, that's not what I was saying at all. I thought you were the cutest girl there, that night. You drank a little bit, and your cheeks turned pink, and you looked *adorable*."

She throws one hand at me, like she's batting my comment away. "Stop."

"I mean it," I say. "If I hadn't needed to push Dave to action, I'd have asked you out."

She meets my eyes for a moment, and then she blushes and looks down at the table. "Here. I'll just take a few more potatoes." She scoops up the green bean bite. "Oh, good. This one has a little bonus."

The girls have been watching us like they watch their tennis balls, their heads whipping back and forth for our entire interchange, but now Ricki leaps in again.

"I can take that," she says.

Barbara shakes her head. "I like to mix my food anyway."

"But that one was in her mouth." Nikki's look of disgust is pretty funny. Especially for two girls who lived surrounded by rats and roaches for so many months.

"It's just extra flavor," Barbara says as she slides it to the side of her plate.

Then we all laugh.

"You're not eating your cranberry sauce?" Barbara

asks, looking pointedly at the maroon blight on my plate.

I poke it. "It makes things look prettier, but it's kind of weird. It's berries that are made into this gelatinous goo."

"Try it on a bite of turkey," Ricki says. "That's how Mom always ate it."

I'm skeptical, but because of who's asking, I try it. "Not bad," I say. "Maybe that's how it's meant to be eaten."

"Sometimes, things are better when you mix them with other things that aren't at all the same," Ricki says. "Mom used to say that."

"Your mom was smart," I say. "I think a lot of things in life are better when they have something else, even something dissimilar, to go along with them." I can't help looking at Barbara, and she blushes. Hopefully she got my meaning.

"Like how we did that promotion for the black bean brownie mix?" Nikki asks.

"Sure," Barbara says. "Although I'm not sure their sales stayed very steady. I think they discontinued that line."

Ricki laughs. "You have such a weird job."

"Do you like it?" Nikki looks genuinely curious.

Barbara—who I thought loved her job—shrugs. "I like that it pays my bills."

"Wait," I say. "You're working at the same place as James, and you don't even like it, but you haven't quit? How many times have I asked you to come work for me?"

"You make it sound like—"

"I always thought you loved your job," I say.

She shrugs. "Some things about it are interesting. I

love helping people like the twins to make some money from doing what they like."

"But you don't like rest of it?"

"Do you like your job?" Ricki asks.

"I *love* my job," I say. "Every single day, I wake up, and I look at broken things, and I fix them. It's literally what I get paid a lot of money to do."

"You fix companies?"

"Exclusively. I used to work with an Investment Bank, and that was cool too, as was the Capital firm I worked for, but in all of those, you're sort of preying on people who are in trouble. I like to help the people who are struggling and then get a really big check for sharing my time."

"Sounds good to me," Nikki says. "Maybe I can do that one day."

"You make it sound like I'm a corporate sell out because I don't love what I do. Most people don't love their jobs," Barbara says. "They just do them because that's how they get paid."

"That's a depressing thought," Bentley says. "If you really think that, and I think that's wrong, then you should reevaluate. You should do something you *love* to do."

"The only thing I like doing is helping people like Ricki and Nikki," Barbara says. "And there's no market for that."

I wipe my mouth. "I'm not sure that's true. You could be an agent."

Barbara frowns. "Why didn't I ever think of that?"

"We don't have an agent," Nikki says. "Or, I don't think we do."

"You don't," Barbara says. "But if you did, you'd have someone whose job it would be to help you find more work."

"But then you'd take our money?" Ricki asks.

"Well, agents get a cut," I say. "But they help you find way more jobs, so you make more overall. They also make sure the contracts are good, so that you don't get stuck doing something you shouldn't."

Barbara's brow furrows. "I had never even considered. . ."

"You should," I say. "I can't even imagine waking up every morning and not being excited to get to work."

She's staring at the same roll she's been holding for at least two minutes. Lucky's staring at it too, but I'm thinking they're staring for different reasons.

"Life's too short to do things you don't want to do," I say.

"What about eating things you don't want to eat?" Ricki asks. "Can we not do that, either?"

I laugh. "Nice try, but if Barbara says you need to eat something, like those brussels sprouts, which are surprisingly good with that glaze. . ."

Ricki groans.

But eventually, we finish dinner and it's time for presents. The girls may have insisted they didn't want any, but now that it's Christmas Eve, they look pretty excited about opening them. I drag four chairs close to the tree, which is in the entryway. I'm just now realizing that it may look nice, but it's a pretty stupid place for a tree. Lucky starts barking and circling like she's not sure what's happening, but she's delighted to be a part of it. That's sort of her modus operandi.

Nikki drops to one knee and starts rubbing Lucky behind her ears. Lucky immediately covers her face with licks, but thankfully it makes Nikki laugh.

"I'm not sure I really want to open any." Ricki's eyes are bright and she's staring right at the pile of gifts.

"Why not?" I ask. "Because if you don't like what's in there, I kept gift receipts, and—"

"I'm sure I'll like them, but I want to have something to open tomorrow." Ricki turns to look at me. "Can I save them?"

I did want to see them open the gifts, but my heart contracts. How could anyone tell that little face no? "Of course you can."

"No, no," Barbara says. "Don't be silly. You'll have more to open tomorrow from Santa. Open these now. I'm sure Bentley will enjoy seeing you open them."

"You first," Ricki says.

"But I actually won't have anything else to open tomorrow," Barbara says. "I should save mine—Santa doesn't come to old people."

"You can save most of yours," I say. "But at least open this." I fish underneath the tree for the smallish box—not the ring box, but still small. I finally find it. "Here."

Barbara rolls her eyes. "Oh, fine. But listen, I've been working a lot, and—"

"He's going to love his gift," Ricki says. "Don't say that yours isn't good."

Barbara arches one eyebrow at Ricki. "It's just that—"

"Just open it," Nikki says.

"You two girls are pretty hard on her," I say. "But I do agree this time." I lean forward a little. "Open it."

Barbara's so careful when she unwraps it, sliding her finger slowly under the tape to release it, and I get a little nervous, because after it's finally open, she just stares at the signed copy of *A Christmas Carol* for a moment. She's frozen, her brow just a little furrowed.

"I know *Pride and Prejudice* is your favorite, but I couldn't find a signed copy of that. I stumbled on this one—the guy I bought all the other books I've gotten you messaged me. They found it in this woman's estate. No one even knew she had it. Apparently when Dickens came to America and did a bunch of readings in 1867, only about a year and a half before he di—"

But she looks up then, and she's crying. "Thank you, Bentley. You always go so far above and beyond anything I could ever—" She sets the book in its box gently and stands up to hug me.

Ricki and Nikki are both smiling when I release her.

I do prevail upon them to open their gifts, and they seem to really like them. I wasn't sure whether nail polish, gift cards for clothing, and matching Nook E-readers with gift cards for books would really be the way to go, but judging from their faces, I did alright.

"And now you open yours," Ricki says.

Barbara shakes her head. "No, he can wait until tomorrow."

My tree's starting to look a little bare—Barbara opened the basket of skincare stuff my assistant insisted she would also love, and the girls just have pairs of matching Ugg boots left underneath there at this point. But my real Christmas is happening tonight, so I'm okay that everything is gone.

I decide to snag the boxes that were wrapped by the girls, and then I rip them open back to back.

"We picked them at the same time," Nikki says.

It's two ties. One is blue, and one is red. "We couldn't decide which one to get—and usually we agree," Ricki says. "But Barbara said we could get both."

I smile. "These are perfect, and for my job, I have to wear a tie every day, so they'll get a lot of wear."

"I told them that," Barbara says.

Before she can stop me, I snag the other box. One from Barbara. I shake it just a bit—because when I'm not rushing, I can't help guessing. There's not much movement, and she knows I dress up for work. "I think it's a dress shirt to go with the ties." I shake it one more time, and then I nod. "It's the right size and weight, and it sounds like fabric."

Barbara's smirking.

So I open it—but it's not a shirt. It's a scarf, and it looks like. . . "Did you make it?" The scarf's kelly green, and on either end, there are two stripes, one smallish cream one, and one thicker red one. The tassel alternates between all three colors.

Barbara always looks so adorable when she blushes. I think that means she did make it herself, which makes me love it even more.

"It's amazing," I say.

"It won't match your style," she says, "but after Mom died, it made me feel better to crochet things. And that one reminded me of you."

"Why?" I ask.

"Because it's green," Ricki says. "Like money."

That makes all of us laugh.

"I think it made me think of those shoes you wore when we first met," she says. "The ones with the stripe?"

It warms my heart a little, thinking that she was paying attention to me, even then.

"Open the other one." She hands me the second box.

It's about the same size as her book box was, and it's about the right weight, too. I catch her eye so I can watch her reaction. "Did you get me a book this year?"

Barbara looks nervous, for some reason, picking at the tissue and wrapping paper she was ignoring before.

Then she starts stacking it all up, like we're going to suddenly start trying to reuse wrapping paper. "Just open it."

"So it's not a book, or you'd be annoyed at my guess." I shake it again. It's sliding a bit—and it's something hard. "Is it a tablet?"

She shakes her head.

"It's a picture?" I ask. "Or maybe a painting?"

"You're ruining the surprise," Ricki says. "Just open it."

I glare at her a bit, but then I finally do open it. It's a photo frame—a beautiful, dark wooden one. And inside, there's a photo of me and Barbara, smiling. She's wearing her gold dress, so it must have been snapped at the holiday party we just attended. I look up at her. "Was this from—"

She's blushing. "Their PR team sent it to me, and I just thought. . ."

It gives me hope. Oliver's stupid words had been rolling around in my head, making me second guess everything. That's why I hid Barbara's last present inside the branches of the tree. But this renews my faith. "Look. I got you something else, too." I reach around her and snag it. Then I set it in her lap.

It's a small blue box.

With a big white bow.

"It's the only gift that didn't match the color scheme," I say, clearly nervous. "That's why it was hiding."

"Is that the only reason?" Nikki asks.

She's an intuitive kid. I shake my head. "I wasn't sure whether I was ready to give it to her," I say slowly.

Barbara has frozen in place, like a beautiful ice sculpture in a garden downtown. "Bentley."

"But I am, so I want you to open it," I say. "And don't get all dramatic."

She blinks, and her hands move slowly, undoing the bow and lifting the lid. But when she sees the cushion-cut diamond, she doesn't beam. She doesn't slide it on her finger, either.

She frowns, which is not promising.

"What is this?"

"It's an engagement ring." I stand up, and then I drop to one knee. "I've known you for fifteen years," I say. "And in that time, I've gotten to know you really well. At first I was going to ask you to date me, because Barbara Champion, I love you."

She's not beaming. "Bentley, I—"

"I know it feels a little sudden, but listen. The more you helped me find someone to date, the more I realized that I only wanted to date you. And then when I thought about dating you, well. You have two little girls you're fostering—adorable, brilliant, talented little girls. You have a lot on your plate. You don't need some wishy-washy guy coming over and being like, 'hey, babe, let's hang out.'"

She laughs. "So you decided *this* would be better?"

That's not exactly the reaction I wanted. "No?" I stand up. "I guess not." It feels like I've been punched in the stomach. Because I don't see any way that this suddenly becomes the yes I was hoping for.

Barbara stands, too. "Bentley, you date someone for a long time before you propose. Do you know why?"

I shake my head, but I can't help feeling like a little boy who just got yelled at for sneaking a cookie.

"Because dating and knowing someone aren't the same. You're putting the cart before the horse here." She hands me the blue box. "I don't think we should get engaged yet, but I would be happy to date you."

"Kind of buried the lead there," I say. "But I guess I'll take it."

It's a little awkward as the girls open their Ugg boots, which they blessedly love, and a little more awkward as I insist they take a lot of the food in to-go boxes for tomorrow, but when Barbara finally heads out the door, she stops in the entry and takes my hand. "I'm sorry that I said no." Her soft smile is kind. "I didn't want to say no, but I think I needed to, for both of us to have a solid start."

That gives me a little hope.

Enough hope that I step closer, grab her hip with one hand, and lean down until my mouth connects with hers. And for the first time in fifteen years, I'm kissing the gorgeous, kind, self-effacing woman that I love.

In that moment, I know that she's wrong. Our start is already as solid as granite bedrock.

But, I'm also okay with waiting for her. I'm alright with her needing to date me first. But I love Barbara Champion right now, and if she'd have said yes, we could be planning our wedding and I wouldn't be a bit unsure about it. After a very brief kiss that I wish was much longer, Barbara steps back.

At least her cheeks are flushed when she says, "Merry Christmas, Bentley."

"I love you, too, Barbara."

She frowns. "I didn't say—"

I smile. "I know what you meant."

She's blushing even more now. But she doesn't correct me. "It's going to be a little hard for me right now," she says. "It's been a really long year."

"I'm in a rush," I say. "I'm not going to lie. But it's only because I can't stand seeing you sad, and I love to see you happy. I plan to make that happen as quickly as possible. But I'm okay with waiting as long as you need."

She nods, but she's smiling.

"And Barbara?"

She blinks.

"Since you turned me down, I'm giving this to you." I slide the ring box into the bag she's carrying.

"That's not how it works," she says.

"Actually, it is," I say. "Because now, when you do want to marry me, you're going to have to propose."

She's laughing when she walks out the door.

I'm watching replays of my favorite football games when my phone rings—and it's Barbara. My heart races, and I answer. "Hello?"

"Hey," a small voice says that is definitely not Barbara.

"Who is this?"

"It's Ricki," the girl says.

"And Nikki. You're on speaker. We're in the bathroom."

"I'm guessing your—er, your foster mom doesn't know you have her phone."

"Definitely not," one of them says. It's really hard to tell without even having their faces to go by.

"Without seeing which of you has her hair back, how will I know who's Ricki?" I realized quickly that was their tell—Ricki's hair is always pulled back. Nikki's is usually down so she can hide her face when she gets nervous.

"It doesn't matter," one of them says.

The other one says, "We just called super quick to tell you this."

Ping pong, it's back to the first. "Look, Barbara just spooks super easy, okay? It's because of that British idiot, but she really does like you."

"I know," I say.

"Oh," one girl says. "Wait, you do?"

"She told me that," I say.

"But really, she loves you too," one of them says. "She talks about you all the time, and when she does, her face gets all weird and she gets all, like, fluttery."

"Fluttery?"

"Like, when her eyelashes are like blinking and she's waving her hands through the air."

I laugh. "And fluttery's good?"

"Very good," one says. "Sometimes when your mom dies, you're just sad, and you need more time to get over it. I think she'll get over it quick."

"Wait, you mean she'll get over losing her mom?"

"Well, yeah, that and her dad and her husband dumping her. It was a bad year."

"I know," I say. "Don't worry. I'm not going anywhere."

And when they hang up, I realize that those girls aren't going anywhere, either. If they're calling me to make sure their foster mom is happy, they already see her as a lot more than a person providing them a hotel room and food.

They see her as their mother, at least a little bit, already.

And that means that if I get my way. . .they'll have a father too. I should be freaking out at the idea, but I'm not. I actually like it. In fact, if Dave weren't on a cruise right now, I'd definitely be calling him for tips.

Me—a dad, with two adorable little girls.

Imagine that.

15

BARBARA

When there's a knock at my door, I peek to make sure it's not Bentley again. When it's Seren, I open it.

"Why does Bentley say you're avoiding him?"

I sigh.

"Seriously? He proposes, and you say no, but you say you'll date him. . .and then for a full week, you duck his calls and text him with lame excuses about being busy?"

"Work has—"

Seren snorts. "No way. Don't even try."

"Look, it's been a bad year for me."

"Yeah, yeah, your mom, your dad, your lousy ex. I've heard it. A *lot*."

I drop into a chair, happy the girls are at tennis. "It's all still true."

"It's an excuse." Seren sits next to me. "A lame one."

"But the thing is, Bentley's so sure," I say. "You didn't see him. He meant it when he proposed, and I have the girls now, and by the way, I called Alice, and she said they found the girls' dad."

Seren lurches forward, her hands bracing on her knees. "Barbara."

"I know." I sigh. "But it seems like good news. He called the state agency in response to a letter that finally reached him. He's been asking a lot of questions about how much money they're making with their Insta account promos, but otherwise seems uninterested in even seeing them. Alice said he's living in California now, and he told her that he can't even afford to come to New York. Apparently he just wanted to confirm that they had a home."

Seren closes her eyes. "That's still bad. In my experience, people like that, once they see there may be money in something, will often not leave. Didn't you say they have a national commercial filming soon?"

I groan. "Yes, but maybe we can buy him off before then."

"You have a lot of money, then, do you?"

Not exactly. "But listen, at least he's not here, demanding that I hand them over."

"I guess." But Seren's unease makes mine flare. "Bentley *does* have a lot of money, you know."

"Yeah, and if that loser knew I was dating him, how greedy do you think he'd get?"

"You're just looking for reasons to back away from this, aren't you?" Seren leans back with a heavy sigh. "Do you really not like him?"

"What's not to like?" I groan. "Of course I like him. I think I might *love* him."

"Then why—" Seren cuts off, her mouth closing with a small click. Then she looks around the family room. "You're sitting in here with the blinds all closed and the curtains drawn."

"Yeah, but that's because at night, people can see

right in the window, and the apartment complex's breezeway is right there." I point.

"There was a time," Seren says slowly, "when I had to take things one day at a time. Sometimes I took things one hour at a time." She taps her lip. "So I get it. The great thing about fostering is that it's always one day at a time. I've been there, too. But Barbara, you can't live your life like that forever." She walks across the room and throws the curtain back. Then she pulls the blinds up.

A very startled man with a phone to his ear stares right at Seren and leaps away, fumbling and nearly dropping his phone.

"See?" I ask.

Seren laughs. "I get your reasoning, but listen to my point." She gestures out the window, and at least the walkway's clear now. "Believing in someone again, after another person has let you down, is scary. It's terrifying, really. James was a real loser, and he's worse because he mostly seems like a decent guy."

"It's not really all his fault," I say. "When Mom died—"

"Save it," Seren says. "He's a selfish jerk."

I chuckle. "Fine."

"You've never been the best about believing in yourself, but your mom and your dad were always there, buoying you up. Now all you have is me to believe in you, and it's not enough. You have to believe in yourself again, too."

"I don't need a pep talk," I say.

"Oh, I disagree. I think you do." Seren points at the window. "See that? That's sunlight. Artificial light just isn't as good. It's not the same. After my parents died, I was afraid to love Dave. I was afraid to be happy at all. It's a normal way to feel after losing someone—and in your case, two someones—you love a lot. But Alice told me then what I'm going to tell you now. You need to welcome the sunshine back into your life, and you need to make the life you want for yourself. Even when it feels like sorrow is the only thing you can see, even when it feels like the dark-ness is where you *belong*, you can't wallow forever in it."

She's right. "Maybe once I do it, I'll be good enough for Bentley."

"Wait," Seren says. "Once you. . .do what?"

"I'm going to quit my job," I say. "I never really wanted to do what I'm doing, and I need to take steps to make my life what it should be. What I deserve."

"Easy there, tiger," she says. "If you need money to pay this loser dad to go away, I'm not sure now's the time to—"

But I've already dialed my boss, and I'm ready to take action. "Hey there," I say when she answers.

And then I give her my two weeks' notice.

"Bonuses are being announced in eight days," my boss says. "Are you sure you don't want to wait a bit."

"Right," I say. "I might have been acting on an impulse. Can we pretend I didn't call?"

"Sure." I can almost hear her smile. "But hold onto that energy. I like it."

"Alright," Seren says after I hang up. "Now, if you're done doing stupid things, how about you call Bentley?"

But I can't bring myself to do it. Not quite.

"I'll call him tomorrow," I say. "I swear."

Seren doesn't want to let it go, I can tell, but she doesn't have a choice.

"I have to go," I say. "The girls have a tennis match. That's why I'm off work today."

"Fine," she says. "But if you don't call him tomorrow, I'm going to come over here and dial his number myself."

"I know." She loves me, so I believe she means it.

"And Barbara." She points. "You have to let the light back in, or things will never get better. Do it. Open the windows."

She's probably right. "But right now, I have no time." I gesture at myself. "Look at me. I can't go to the game like this."

"Match," Seren says. "Tennis has matches."

"Whatever," I say.

After she finally leaves, I close the windows—not symbolically, but because I don't like the people walking by being able to peer inside. And then I throw my hair up into a quick and dirty bun, and I change into something that's not yoga pants, and I head for the tennis *match*.

I'm barely able to find a seat before it starts.

Only, when I start to cheer for the cutest doubles team ever, someone else behind me is cheering even louder than I am. For a moment I panic. Is it their dad?

But when I turn around, it's not.

It's Bentley.

I inadvertently kick a woman in the nose climbing up to the top row of the bleachers—what is he doing up so high?—but when I get there, I'm irritated. "Why are you here?"

"Me?" Bentley touches his broad chest, with clearly visible musculature even under his stupidly fancy sweater. "Oh, I'm just low-key stalking this woman I'm in love with. She said she loved me too—"

"No, I didn't. I said Merry Christmas."

But now he's cheering again.

"They scored," he says.

I force myself to pay attention to the match, but

it's hard when Bentley's knee keeps bumping mine. I glance sideways.

"What?" he asks. "Have you ever been a huge guy on bleachers?" He's whispering, but the woman next to me is staring at him like he's a famous movie star. "Because it's not easy. Sorry if I'm accidentally touching you."

"He can touch me any time he wants," the lady next to me mutters.

"What?" Bentley asks.

"Nothing," I hiss. "But listen, I didn't say—"

"Merry Christmas," Bentley says, his words so loaded they're practically dripping, "*Barbara*."

Okay. I maybe see his point. "But still, all I said was—"

"You said we could date," he says. "You said I could take you out. That I'd be your boyfriend."

The woman next to me has eyes as round as tennis balls. "That's your boyfriend?"

I roll my eyes.

"Because he's a real upgrade."

"Excuse me?"

"It was the British guy before, right?"

Who *is* this woman? "I'm sorry," I say. "Do I know you?"

"You're Killian's aunt, aren't you?" The woman blinks. "I thought I'd seen you at the high school games."

I forget, for a moment, how many kids' things I've been to over the years. "Oh, no, that's me."

"I thought so, and trust me." She tosses her head. "Better. Way better."

I can't help laughing. "That's true."

"See?" Bentley says. "Give the people what they want."

I can't help my half smile. And when the match is over, and Bentley insists on taking us out for ice cream, even when it's twenty-nine degrees, I don't argue. Then, when the girls want him to build a snowman now that it's finally snowed, I don't argue with him about that, either.

And when he shows up for every tennis match, and we start going to ice cream after every single one, I don't complain. Because I suppose, when you have two foster daughters, this is what dating is.

When he starts bringing dinner over most days, and joining us on others, when either the girls or I have cooked, I don't argue with that. When Alice calls to tell me that their father agreed to sign papers to terminate his parental rights, as long as the government doesn't pursue any child support from him, it feels like things in my life can't get any better. But they do. Before I know it, we're all seeing Bentley every single day. The girls shoot their commercial, albeit a little later than the gum people wanted, and it goes over really well when it launches.

Everything in my life is looking brighter and better, and after I manage to hire someone to take my place, my manager even wishes me well in my departure. So it makes sense that, when my car is in the shop and I have to take the bus, Bentley comes to pick me up with a smile and a bouquet of flowers.

"For the best agent in New York," he says.

"I have exactly zero clients," I say. "I'm pretty sure I'm the worst."

"Well, you have the girls, at least," he says.

"Think again," I say. "I can't represent them since I'm their foster mom, and I couldn't take them either way. They're excluded by the non-compete I signed since I met them through the firm."

He grimaces. "Well, still. You have a lot of potential, kid."

"At first, that non-compete that kept me from even looking for clients scared me. I have savings, but not a ton. With plans for the girls adoption under way. . .I was stressed. It's not like that's going to look great on a home report."

"But now?"

"They need me a lot right now, and I've never loved my job. The reason I'm leaving is that I want to do something good. Something fulfilling. Something I'll be proud of, and if that takes a little time and depletes my savings a little, I'm not going to stress about it."

"You don't have to worry about money, either," Bentley says. "You do know that, right?"

"I know, and you have no idea how much I appreciate your willingness to help us. But it's actually been knowing that you'll support me emotionally, no matter what I do or how long it takes that has made me feel safe."

"Well, then I hope you'll let me take you to dinner and tell you about all the ways I plan to support you." He's beaming.

"Telling me all the ways sounds great, but I'm on a diet," I remind him. Even though I haven't lost a single pound for the past month, and I've been on a diet the whole time.

"Diet schmiet," he says. "Some days need to be celebrated."

"Like all the days the girls win at tennis?" I ask. "And the day they shot their commercial?"

"And your birthday next week," he says. "And Tuesdays. Sundays too, probably."

I'm smiling, but he really is making it hard for me to lose any weight. "I know you mean well, but—"

"You look amazing right now," he says. "And I will support your diet if you insist, but I don't think you need it."

I realize, as I stare at his very earnest face. . .that he means it. He's not just saying it because he thinks he should. Something inside of me eases in that moment, because if Bentley means it, maybe I can stop being so hard on myself too.

"Merry Christmas, Barbara."

I roll my eyes out of habit.

But he's right—I did love him at Christmas, but I couldn't say it. Even now, it's a little hard for me to say *I love you*, but I can always say Merry Christmas, and we both know what it means for us. Every time he says it, it makes me smile, even when my eyes are welling with tears. "Merry Christmas to you, too, Bentley."

He leans across the center console and kisses me then, quickly, and it feels like coming home.

"By the way," he says. "Your birthday present came in early. Did you want it now? Or on your birthday?"

I'm a woman. Once I know about something. . . "Now, obviously."

When he pulls out a box, my heart skips a beat. "Bentley."

"I told you." He shakes his head. "I'm not proposing again. You have to do that, and you better do a good one."

I laugh.

He hands me the box, and I realize it's a bit larger than a ring box.

"Is this a—"

He snatches it back. "Ah, ah, ah, you aren't supposed to guess. I got in trouble for that at Christmas."

I roll my eyes, but I open it. "Keys?" I pull them

out, and I notice the keychain is a woman sitting on Santa Claus's lap. It says "Naughty *and* Nice?" I can't help laughing at that. "What are these keys for?" But I can see the logo on the car key—it says Land Rover.

He shrugs. "I got myself a Land Rover last week, because I didn't have anything with a solid five seats."

"Five?" I lift my eyebrows. "Did one of your exes turn up pregnant?"

He laughs. "Not a chance. But I figure the girls might want to bring a friend somewhere one day, and I should have room. While I was buying myself the red one—"

"Such an obnoxious color."

He leans over and presses a kiss to my cheek. "I'm an obnoxious guy, in case you hadn't noticed. But you *wish me a Merry Christmas* anyway."

I laugh, because he's saying that I love him anyway. And I do.

"Don't worry. When they told me that Land Rovers were buy one, get a Range Rover free, I told them I needed bright yellow for you."

"What?" I look around, frantically, and there's not a Red Land Rover in sight.

But there is a bright, electric blue Range Rover. And when I press the unlock button, the lights on it flash. "You're kidding."

"About the buy one get one free?" He sighs and nods. "Sadly, yes. I had to pay full price."

I can't help smiling. "Bentley, this is not a normal birthday present."

"Well, that's fine. I'm not a normal guy, and you, my dear, are not a normal girl. You're *my* birthday girl."

I should tell him no.

I know that I should turn him down, but instead, I'm beaming the whole way to the school where I pick up the girls, glancing back at where Bentley's following me the entire way. When they get in the car, the girls are nearly as giddy as I am about it. They must take a dozen photos each of the inside on our way back to the apartment.

"Bentley's amazing," Ricki says. "I mean, this car is just. . ." She shakes her head.

"Why does it smell so good?" Nikki asks. "Like, what is that?"

"It's new car smell, dummy," Ricki says.

"I think it's the leather," I say, still a little in awe myself.

"I'm glad you took the present," Nikki says. "Knowing you, I'd have thought you'd turn him down."

"I considered it," I admit, "but he seemed so happy about it. And I was thinking, it's probably not too bad to take a car from someone. . .when you're planning to marry them."

Ricki squeals first.

But Nikki's not far behind.

"You're going to propose?" Ricki asks.

"Finally," Nikki says.

"It is about time," Ricki says. "How are you going to do it?"

"I was thinking maybe you girls would have some ideas," I say. "Not to put it off on you, but I'd like you to be involved if you want. After all. . ."

"He'll be our dad," Ricki says, and she's smiling.

"He's the nicest guy ever," Nikki says. "And you already turned him down, so the proposal needs to be really good."

"What about Valentine's Day?" Ricki asks. "Since he proposed on Christmas?"

"That's in two days," I say. "It's a little quick."

"Well, it's not our fault you took forever to decide."

"Forever?" I laugh. "It's been less than seven weeks."

"Still." Ricki leans forward, dropping a hand on the back of my chair. "You've known him for fifteen years, and hey, we turn twelve soon. If he gave you a car, what do you think he'll get us?"

"Oh, stop," Nikki says.

"You're not worried that the sky will fall if something good happens?" I'm teasing them, but I'm actually really happy that they've stopped being so nervous about good fortune. "I'm really glad you both like him."

"I do," Nikki says. "But even so, maybe I'm a little nervous."

"Nothing bad happened after Christmas," I say. "You have nothing to worry about." As I say that, I feel a little twinge of fear. Alice hasn't sent the paperwork from their dad yet, but she said he hasn't shown the least bit of interest in coming out here, so I'm sure it's fine.

They have nothing to worry about, and neither do I, I remind myself.

But when we walk up the sidewalk to the apartment, there's a man waiting for us at the door. He's pacing, and he looks. . .nervous. "Hello?" I ask.

"No." Ricki stops moving, balling up her hands at her side. She drops her tennis bag on the ground.

Nikki ducks behind me without a word, crouching over. Her whimper is so quiet that I barely hear it.

"Hey girls," the man says. "It's so good to see you again. Thanks to a bit of luck, Daddy's finally home."

16

BENTLEY

I'm not a violent person.

In fact, in more than forty years, I've only punched someone else on three occasions, outside of a sparring ring. That's not *never*, but given the sheer number of obnoxious jerks I've met in my life, I feel like it shows that I know how to exercise restraint. One of them was actually trying to steal a woman's purse, so I feel like that one doesn't really count.

When I follow Barbara home, there's a strange man waiting. A man with a combover—which is something I didn't think anyone did anymore—and very shiny, very hard looking shoes.

"Looks like the new car drives alright," I say as I walk toward Barbara's apartment, slowly.

"It was great," Barbara says, but she doesn't turn to face me. She's staring at the man like he's a viper, poised to strike.

Both of the girls are hiding behind her too, which isn't a good sign. Nikki's literally right behind Barbara, her head ducked down so no part of her shows other than her sneakers. And Ricki's glaring at the man from over Barbara's shoulder.

"That shiny new blue one?" the man asks. "Was it a gift?"

"It was a gift," I say, "from her boyfriend." I hold out my hand. "Bentley Harrison."

"I'm Patrick Creecher, Nicole and Racquel's dad."

"Racquel?" I turn to look at Ricki.

"I hate that name," she says.

"Oh, come now," Patrick says. "That's my mother's name."

"She was worse than you," Ricki says, her eyes flashing. "Why are you here?"

"Apparently you need to be taught a few lessons in respect," the man says.

A very strong urge comes over me then, to punch my fourth man. "How about you teach me some lessons?" I jerk my thumb back at my car. "And I'll buy you some dinner while you do it."

"I'm not here to talk to you," he says. "I'm here to talk to my girls."

"I see that," I say. "But I think you'll want to talk to me first."

The man grimaces, sliding his hand over the top of his head and pushing his very thin, very greasy hairs to the side to tuck them behind his ear. "Fine." He turns. "But then I want to see my girls. They better be ready to give their old man a big hug and kiss when we get back."

I wouldn't count on it, buster.

"Maybe just order a pizza," I say over my shoulder as we walk back toward the parking lot.

"Is that the kind of food you've been feeding them?" Patrick shakes his head. "Not a very balanced diet."

Why is it that the people who are the very worst at caring for the people they should love are the most critical of the people doing a good job? My hand's literally twitching to teach him some manners, but I'm pretty sure it's not time yet. "What kind of food do you like?" I ask. "I'm happy to take you to get soup and salad anywhere you'd like."

He scoffs. "Steak. Steakhouses have nice salads, right?"

"Sure," I say.

I drive to the Benjamin Steakhouse, since it's close, but I almost hate taking him here. "How about this?"

"It looks alright." He straightens his shoulders like he's a part of the royal family. "I suppose it'll do."

He doesn't ask about the girls. He doesn't tell me where he's been. He doesn't say anything at all, except to criticize the floors, the lighting, and the tables. But once we have menus, he peruses his, sets it down, and steeples his hands.

"I hear my girls been making lots of money for you lately."

That takes me by surprise. "They haven't made a dime for me," I say. "And I know for a fact that Barbara isn't taking any money from them either."

He leans toward me. "Then where—"

But the waiter shows up. We place our orders—he gets the biggest filet on the menu, with two extra sides and two desserts. It's clear that he's not planning to pay.

"Alright, when the waiter came, you had a question for me."

"Yes. I want to know where all the money they're getting paid is going, if you aren't taking it."

I lean back in my chair. "They're paid for the

promos they do on their Insta page, and I think they were paid fairly well for the commercial they did."

"I seen it. That's a big gum company, so I know they paid real good."

"You haven't seen your girls for at least three years."

"But they're good girls, and I'm their dad."

"Yes, I know that both things are true." Miraculously. They look nothing like him. "But you haven't asked me how they're doing in school, or how they're doing in tennis, and you haven't—"

"They're playing tennis?" He lifts his eyebrows. "Their mom played tennis in high school."

"Yes, well, they're doubles partners, and they're very good at it."

"Maybe there's a tennis company that might want—"

"What do you want, Mr. Creecher? Why are you here?"

He smiles slowly. "I like you, Mr. Harrison. I like how you don't beat around the bushes. You get right to the point."

"And what is the point?"

"I got some papers from the government wanting me to sign away my rights to those girls, and at first I thought that was smart. I been worried for years that they might come after me."

"After you?"

"The government, I mean, and when I heared that their mom passed, then I really worried."

I'm going to do it. I'm going to punch him. "So you did hear their mother died."

He nods slowly. "She mighta called me a time or two before then, but I wasn't in a place to watch them, mind you. I just wasn't, and I knew she wanted money.

That woman always wanted money. She didn't even spend none of it on those girls."

I grit my teeth.

"Anyhow, I was about to sign those papers, and then it hit me. They're coming after me to get me to sign *now*, because those girls must be making some real hooch."

I blink. "Some. . .what?" Is he saying they're making alcohol? "I'm not sure what you're saying."

He leans forward. "They're making money, Mr. Harrison, and I know it. Right after I *didn't* sign them papers, I turned on a show on my phone, and guess what I saw?"

"Their commercial?"

He slams his hand down on the table and grins, and I realize he's missing a few teeth in the back. "That's right. I saw their commercial, and I realized that old Patrick nearly got hoodwinked."

Hoodwinked. Yeah, there's no getting one over on old Patrick.

"Do you have the papers right now?" I ask.

"Sure do." He pulls them out of his backpack, smoothing them out with a dirty hand, which adds a small streak down the front. "But before I came out here, I called that Alice lady, and I told her I wanted some money if I was gonna sign these, and she asks me all sharp-like if Barbara offered me money."

"What did you tell her?" I hope Barbara didn't offer him anything.

"I'm no dope. I told her Barbara ain't offered me nothing yet, but I wasn't gonna sign without it."

"Of course you did."

"But she says that if I sign them after getting money from Barbara, then Barbara can't keep the girls. And that's when I realized what was going on."

"You did?"

He nods and smiles even bigger. "Yep, see, she's in on it. That foster woman knows that Barbara likes my girls, and she knows they're making a mint right now. So she doesn't want me to get any of it."

"Mister Creecher, what amount are you here to demand? Because I am not Barbara, and I can pay you, if that's what it takes to get those forms signed."

"And you got money, because you just bought that Range Rover." His smile gives me chills.

"I do have money, yes."

"I knew it. I just knew when I saw you, that you was a smart man."

It's a miracle those girls are as lovely and as kind and as wonderful as they are, since they come in some part from this. "I am a smart man."

I text my office manager and tell her to come here immediately.

Then I refocus on the sleaze. "I'm smart enough that I'm not going to pay you to sign those papers. You're going to sign them because it's the right thing to do."

Mr. Creecher stands up, clearly ready to protest, but our salads arrive, as well as a basket of bread, and I guess he's not quite ready to walk away. "Look here," he says, once the waiter is gone. "I know what those girls are worth, and I'm not budging."

He's actually trying to *sell* them to me. I'm not sure what to say.

"The way I see it, I'm offering you a sweet discount."

"A discount?" I'm worried I won't be able to stop myself. "What on earth does that mean?"

"I know full well that they'll make you a lot of money between now and when they turn eighteen, and

I know you need to make some kinda profit, but I'm in a bind, see, and I need my cut now. I know that means I won't get quite as much in the long run, but you'll have the hassle of feeding them and buying them little duds to wear. So I feel like this is fair."

"What amount, *exactly*, do you feel is fair?"

"Two hundred thousand dollars," he says. "I know they got paid twenty grand for that commercial, cuz I called the company, and the lady let it spill."

"She did."

He nods. "So if they just do ten more commercials like that, you've gotten your money back."

"But what about taxes?" I ask. "And their food and clothing is expensive. Not to mention the rent on an apartment, cars for them to drive, phones to use, etcetera. And there's no guarantee they'll get more commercials. Up until now, it's just been a few hundred here and there for doing little videos on Instagram."

Mr. Creecher's smile is predatory. "Well, you'll just have to decide if you think they're worth the invest-ment, I suppose. If they ain't, I'm willing to risk it myself."

That thought makes my blood run cold.

"I assume you have a checking account," I say.

"You wanna make monthly payments?" He nods slowly. "Well, we could maybe—"

"No," I say. "But I won't pay you to sign the papers, as I mentioned."

"Why not?" he asks. "If I sign these, you and that lady can adopt them. That's what Alice said."

"Whether Barbara adopts them or not is her busi-ness," I say. "I'm just the boyfriend, but what I will pay you to do is apologize."

"Apologize. . ." He frowns. "I don't understand."

I whip out my phone. "Tell me you have internet banking."

Mr. Creecher nods. "I do. Course."

"Well, after you swear to me that you're going to apologize to those girls, you're going to sign these papers in front of a notary public. My office manager will be here momentarily. You're going to testify to her that you're not being paid to do it. Do you understand me?"

Mr. Creecher frowns.

"And then, when she leaves, and the papers are in her care, you're going to call on my phone and apologize to those girls for not being here when you heard their mother was sick. You're going to tell them you're sorry that you haven't been in their life, and you're going to promise that you won't drag them down any more."

"Now, wait just a second," he says. "I woulda come if I coulda, but I had a lot going on in my life, and there was no way—"

"And then as soon as you've done that," I say, "I will transfer two hundred thousand dollars into your account via my phone wire transfer app here. See?" I show him my account balance so he knows I can, and then I show him the transfer option. "And then, after that, you and I will never have another interaction. Are we clear?"

Our steaks arrive then, but by the time we've finished eating them, my office manager's arrived, and Mr. Creecher does exactly as I told him to do. He signs the forms, and he insists, while my brilliant office manager video tapes him, that he wasn't paid to sign. Once I have his notarized, unconditional surrender of parental rights, I feel much, much lighter. The only hiccup is that Barbara doesn't answer when I call, so he's forced to leave his apology on her voicemail. I decide that's good enough. They can replay it as many times as they want.

And then, I transfer him the money.

While I'm paying the check for dinner, the man practically dances around—the clearance of funds has already come through on his phone. "You're an interesting guy." He laughs. "Actually, for someone so rich, you're really stupid."

"Is that so?" I walk out of the restaurant while he trots along behind me, smiling ear to ear.

"It is," he says. "Your girlfriend must not tell you anything at all, because I lied to you, and you didn't even know it."

My stomach drops. Is he not really the girls' father? Did he just sign forms that don't really free those girls? I feel a little sick. Losing the money's frustrating, but is there still some kind of piranha out there, waiting to try and bite those little girls? Waiting to attack Barbara?

"You really should talk to your girlfriend more." He's grinning very obnoxiously. It's almost as bad as the Joker in Batman. "And there's such a thing in the world known as *haggling*."

"Haggling?" I'm really confused.

He starts to laugh so hard that he has tears running down his face. "Two hundred thousand dollars." He shakes his head. "What an idiot."

"Why am I an idiot?" I ask. "Because I still happen to think that's a bargain to free those girls from someone like you."

"I lied about that commercial. They only made five grand." He wipes his eyes. "You, sir, were just duped."

And that's it.

I've hit my limit.

I ball up my fist and I punch the man right on the nose. I feel the crunch, so I know it's good and broken. And that makes me grin even bigger than he just was. "Well, now we're even. I gave you a big pile of money you don't deserve, but you're the real idiot. I'd have paid ten times as much, and you were too stupid to know it."

He crumples into a heap on the ground, his hands covering his nose.

I crouch down beside him. "Ever heard of negotiation? The most fundamental principle of business is to know the value of what you have." I stand. "And if you ever think about coming after me again, you should know that I have the best investigative team in the United States. They've already sent me three emails about you, with things they uncovered just during the time we were at dinner. One is a DUI you ran from in Alabama. One's an assault charge on a misdemeanor in Tennessee. And one is charges pending against you for something to do with the disappearance of Jacqueline Pierce. Believe me when I say that if I ever see you again, Mr. Creecher, you'll also be dealing with the authorities. And I'll be sure to tell them how you extorted me for two hundred grand. Who do you think they'll believe?"

When I walk away from Mr. Creecher, for what I assume will be the last time, I can't help walking with a spring in my step. My hand might sting a bit, but overall, I feel really, really good.

17

BARBARA

I'm not great at surprising people. In high school, I tried to surprise Seren with a trip to the beach. Only, during gym class, I noticed she had a swimsuit in her bag.

"Hey," I said. "Why do you have a swimsuit?"

"You asked me about five things about the beach last week, so when my mom told me I should pack a bag to stay at your house this weekend, I kind of figured I'd need it."

When I tried to surprise my parents on their anniversary, Mom walked into the party with full makeup on and her hair done.

"She knew," I said to Dad.

He chuckled. "You left one of the invites in your car."

I closed my eyes. "And she picked it up from the oil change place."

I just can't ever manage to keep all the details from leaking. It's not my forte. But this time, I'm pretty sure I've kept the cat entirely tied up in that bag.

I've never really gotten that phrase, because, like,

who wants to keep a cat in a bag? Wouldn't it die? No one wants a dead cat, right? But anyway, I've done it. I've got a dead cat this time—I'm almost certain.

"Why is Bentley in court?" Ricki's rummaging around in her backpack, looking for who knows what.

"Look, I told you guys that we're going to the beach, but—"

"But he doesn't know," Nikki says. "You've already said, like eight times."

"Well, he had some work he had to do, and part of it was at the courthouse, so this is where Oliver said he'd be."

"Going to the beach to celebrate is cool, but proposing at the courthouse is kind of lame," Nikki says. "You should've done that restaurant he likes."

"Yeah," Ricki says. "Courthouses are for depressing things, like being told that you're being placed in a new home or, like, getting a divorce." Ricki finally finds her lip gloss, and she punches her hand into the air over her head.

"Can we finally go in?" I ask. "I told you already—meeting him at the courthouse gives us a perfect excuse to dress really nice. He won't have any inclination that I'm going to propose. He'll think we're here for a routine custody hearing or something, and he won't be suspicious."

"I guess," Nikki says. "But it's still a little annoying."

As we're walking toward the front door, Seren and Dave amble up.

"What are you two doing here?" I hiss.

"You thought we'd miss this?" Seren asks. "You came to ours." She glances at the girls with big eyes.

"Oh my gosh," Nikki says. "You invited the whole world."

"It's only my best friend," I'm saying, when I see Emerson, Elizabeth, Killian, Ardath, and Bea walking toward us. "Seren," I hiss.

"I'm sorry," she says, "but when Bea heard—"

"Hey, Aunt Barbara." Elizabeth glances at the girls. "I heard Uncle Bentley was going to be inside?"

"Look," Nikki says. "If you all show up, he'll *know* right away that she's here to propose."

And of course, Killian bursts out laughing. I want to kick him.

"Shut up, all of you," I say. "The girls and I are going in first, and the rest of you can come later. Okay?"

No one argues, and we all stroll inside.

"I don't understand," Nikki says. "If they all show up, even if they come after Uncle Bentley's done with his trial or whatever, how will he not immediately realize—"

But we've reached the courthouse doors, and I press hard enough to open them both at once. It's a little sad that Nikki, at eleven, already knows that once they open, if court's in session, she has to be quiet.

"Ah, the ladies of the day are here," the judge says.

Nikki's and Ricki's eyes widen, and their heads swivel toward me. "Surprise," I say.

"What's going on?" Ricki asks.

"We thought you might like to be here today," I say, "you know, for your formal adoption hearing."

"For—what?" Nikki starts to sob.

Ricki tackles me, nearly knocking me over.

"But before the adoption," I say, "I wanted to ask you something."

"Me?" the judge says.

I shake my head, and after it becomes clear that I'm utterly unable to dislodge Ricki from her place around my waist, I just start walking, dragging her along like a very closely adhered barnacle. "I had a quick question for the younger Mr. Harrison, Your Honor."

The judge, Bentley's father, is smiling. "Go right ahead."

"You already know the question," I say to the judge. "Because I called last week to ask your permission to propose to your son." And then I pull a ring out of my pocket. "This isn't a Tiffany's ring, because unlike your son, I can't afford Tiffany's."

Bentley's staring right at me, and he's already beaming.

"I found this company called Staghead Designs, and they make the coolest wedding bands. It started with this family who made bands out of things they had around their property. Barn hinges. Old trees. Things that had meaning to those people in particular. Well, I had my parents' wedding bands, which were both very simple, melted down, and they made them into a design they call fire-treated distressed, with a seascape finish."

I hold out the box, and he takes it.

"You'll see that the finish isn't smooth and shiny. It's a little rough, and a little weathered, just like me."

Ricki has popped her head away from my side, finally, and she's watching carefully. Nikki's staring, too. She's followed us along, like a little duckling trailing its mother. "I thought there might not be a better day than today to propose to you. Without you, I might not have recovered from losing my parents. Without you, I might not believe my happily ever after was ever coming. And without you, I might not have trusted that anyone would ever want the three of us—beautiful, but battered souls."

"But I do want you. All three of you." Bentley looks

behind me. "Which is why your foster mom asked me to come today. She told me that the two of us could adopt the two of you. If you'll have us."

Nikki nods slowly, and Ricki beams. She detaches herself from me, and tackle-hugs Bentley.

"I'll take that as a yes," Bentley says. "And I'm hoping that you're okay with my dad being the judge for the final hearing."

"Of course," I say. "But you never answered my question."

"I need my ring back to do that."

I pull it out of my bag. "I thought you might want it."

Bentley pulls the blue lid off. "The moment I saw this ring in that store, I knew that I wanted you to have it. And I knew that I wanted to have you. Forever."

"So that's a yes?" I ask.

Bentley nods. "That's a *heck* yes. And also, Merry Christmas, to the future Mrs. Harrison."

"You know it's like, way past Christmas, right?" Killian asks.

"Hush," Seren says. "It's their thing."

"And for the record, that went *way* better than mine did," Dave says from the back row.

The entire Fansee family starts to clap, then.

"You invited them all?" Bentley asks.

I shrug. "Not so much, but they don't really wait for an invite."

Bentley wraps one arm around my shoulders, and Nikki nestles in on his other side, by her barnacle sister. "Real family rarely does."

"Well, I don't feel as bad for crashing either, then." Bentley's mother ducks her head out from the door to the judge's chambers, and she's smiling.

And I notice for the first time that my future mother-in-law really is quite a heavy woman. I've known her for years. We've met three or four times at various large events, and I never once noticed that she's the same size as I am.

Bentley was telling the truth.

Maybe he really doesn't mind that I haven't lost any weight yet. Maybe he loves me just as I am. He's sliding the wedding band on his finger, and I stop him. "Hey, you're not supposed to wear that yet."

He tucks my ring in his pocket. "Oh, I don't know about that. The person who proposes doesn't wear one —the person who says yes does."

Ricki lets go of him and straightens. "No, it's the woman who's supposed to wear an engagement ring."

"Are you sure?" Bentley arches one eyebrow, but he pulls my ring back out and offers it to me. "How about we compromise?"

"What do you mean?" I ask.

"We can both wear one."

"What about us?" Nikki asks. "Why don't we get anything?"

"I think," Judge Harrison says, "that after this is over, my wife and I should take you shopping and let you each pick one, too."

Bentley's mom claps. "Shopping with my grand-daughters? This is the best day ever."

"That sounds like a win win," Bentley says.

Mrs. Harrison leans over the judge's stand. "I hope you girls are ready to be spoiled. I've been waiting for you for a very long time.."

Bentley looks relieved, like he had no idea how his mother would react. It makes me a little sad that my mom's not here. I know she'd be over the moon.

Spending time with me was her greatest joy, always.. "I think Nikki and Ricki could use a little spoiling."

"Two of the loveliest girls I've ever seen, and now they're my grandchildren," Mrs. Harrison says. "Just wait until my friends find out. They'll be so jealous."

Judge Harrison clears his throat. "Maybe we give Bentley and Barbara and the girls a little social space for now."

Mrs. Harrison frowns, but she walks to the side and sits down. "Alright, well, carry on."

And after that, Judge Harrison and our lawyer prove up the adoption, and Nikki and Ricki become our daughters. And in a few months, Bentley and I will stand in front of a pastor, and we'll become spouses.

But to be honest, that'll be extra.

Because our family feels pretty darn complete right in this moment.

*** I hope you LOVED Minted. If you're wondering about the REST of their story—wedding, etc., don't! This will be like my Finding Home series. I will have their wedding in the NEXT book, Loaded, which is Bea's book! So hang on, and very soon, you'll get to read more about Bentley and Barbara. <3

As a special incentive to join my newsletter, I did write a rather long BONUS chapter that shows how Beatrice joined the Fansee family. It has Dave, Seren, and Emerson, and I think you might really enjoy reading it. It's EXCLUSIVE—you can only get it if you join my newsletter here.

Loaded is coming early in 2024. I hope you're as excited to read about Emerson's sister Bea as I am to write it.

. . .

LOADED
THE CARSDALE FOSTERS
B.E. BAKER

ACKNOWLEDGMENTS

Thank you to my husband, my kids, and my editor. I always thank all of you, and I always mean it. From the bottom of my heart.

A huge thank you also to all my readers. Without you, I could not have this job that I love. And you are such amazing people. You bring me so much joy. Thank you for your reviews, your shares, your recommendations, and your excitement.

I have animals coming out of my ears. Seven horses. Three dogs, three cats, thirty-ish chickens. I'm always doctoring or playing with an animal... and I wouldn't want it any other way. But Leo (my palomino) is still my very favorite.

When I'm not with animals, or even if I am, I'm likely to have at least one of my five kids in tow, two of which I'm currently homeschooling.

My hubby is the reason all this glorious madness is possible. He's the best parts of all the amazing men I write (although he's bald and his six pack sometimes goes into hiding because of cookies.)

I also love to bake, like to cook, and feel amazing when I find time to kickbox, lift weights, or rollerblade. Oh yeah, and I'm a lawyer, but I try to forget about that whenever I can.

I adore my husband, and I love my God.

The rest is just details.

The Setback

The Lookback

Children's Picture Book

Yuck! What's for Dinner?

B. E. Baker writes FANTASY ROMANCE and other stories
with speculative elements under Bridget E. Baker (her real
name!)

**The Dragon Captured Series: (dragon shifter
romance!)**

Ensnared

Entwined

Embroiled

Embattled

The Russian Witch's Curse: (horse shifter romance!)

My Queendom for a Horse

My Dark Horse Prince

My High Horse Czar

My Wild Horse King

The Magical Misfits Series: (paranormal humor!)

Mates: Minerva (1)

Mates: Xander (2)

The Birthright Series: (urban fantasy romance)

Displaced (1)

unForgiven (2)

Disillusioned (3)

misUnderstood (4)

Disavowed (5)

unRepentant (6)

Destroyed (7)

The Birthright Series Collection, Books 1-3

The Anchored Series: (urban fantasy romance)

Anchored (1)

Adrift (2)

Awoken (3)

Capsized (4)

The Sins of Our Ancestors Series: (dystopian romance)

Marked (1)

Suppressed (2)

Redeemed (3)

Renounced (4)

Reclaimed (5) a novella!

A stand alone YA romantic suspense:

Already Gone

www.ingramcontent.com/pod-product-compliance
Lightning Source LLC
Chambersburg PA
CBHW020804190726
48285CB00006B/2162